BETTING ON HER

A WILDE LOVE NOVEL

KELLY COLLINS

For all the girls who love bad boys.

CHAPTER ONE

On the second floor balcony, I looked at the gardens below. Red and yellow roses in full bloom scented the air with sweetness and sorrow. My mother loved her roses. Loved them so much, she dove from this exact spot into them. If I closed my eyes, I could still see her lifeless body in the midst of their beauty.

My father's Italian loafers tapped across the tile entry floor downstairs, the sound echoing through the grand foyer. The massive front door slammed behind him. Russian spewed from his mouth like a dam let loose after a storm. Little did he know, the storm was just beginning. I was a tempest in training, and my rage and hurt swirled around me like a hurricane—like a class three storm building to a disastrous five.

I raced from the room I'd been forbidden to enter since my mother died seventeen years ago. I'd only recently found the key hidden in the soil of a nearby potted plant. Our housekeeper Darya stared straight at me one day while she buried it in the dirt.

"Your father doesn't want you inside her room." She looked over her shoulder to make sure no one was watching or listening. "I don't think a child should be kept from her mother, living or dead, and this room is all that's left of her." She raised her finger to her lips in a silent "shh."

With my shoes in my hand, I tiptoed down the hallway. I'd barely made it to my bedroom door when he bellowed, "Katya, come meet your future husband."

"I'll be right there," I called in my sweetest voice while I slid on my heels and belted a knife to my thigh.

If I could help it, Sergei Volkov would never be my husband. His reputation preceded him. Said to be handsome but deadly, he was the kind of man no one considered lightly. Why my father had chosen him, I couldn't say. Maybe he hadn't, and the Russian mafia placed Sergei here. Even though my father ran the business in Las Vegas, the Bratva ran him.

Was Sergei my punishment for not getting Alex Wilde to the altar? Something told me the punishment wasn't meant for me, but my father. In the end, I'd pay the price for his failures. I was a girl and had no value except in trade. On the felt of a poker table, I'd be the hundred-dollar chip. My worth was little, unless I could be played to increase the odds of winning the long game.

There was no doubt the homeland sent Sergei, which meant the Russian Brotherhood wasn't pleased with how my father ran things in Sin City. How could they be? He'd lost his alliance with the Wildes when Alex married Faye. Add to that the death of Dima, his second in command, and my brother going to prison, and it didn't paint a picture of a man capable of running anything.

Sergei had come to Las Vegas to gamble, and I was the initial wager. My father offered me up like a complementary room at a high-end casino.

My stilettos click-clacked across the marble floor. I chanced a glance over the iron railing to see if my future handler was visible. There he stood, no less than six feet tall, with shoulders so broad, he must have had to walk through the door sideways. Happy to have this one moment to take him in without notice, I cataloged everything I could about him. If Shrek and Dwayne Johnson had a baby, I was certain he'd look like Sergei. Shrek's build, Dwayne's looks. While I liked big, imposing men, this man scared the hell out of me. Dressed all in black from his perfectly pressed dress shirt to his wingtip leather shoes, he portrayed the villain well.

I recognized evil when I saw it. It was always in the eyes. Eyes that held no life. Showed no joy. Never delivered an ounce of compassion. I'd lived under the power and control of my father for nearly twenty-five years, and now my leash would be transferred to a man known for cruelty.

When my mother was alive, things were different. Her love softened our hard life. She was sunshine and happiness and joy, but for the last seventeen years, I'd lived in the shadow of darkness. I both hated and loved my mother for what she did, but I could never understand how a woman with two children could be so selfish to take her life and leave us here to fend for ourselves. Now I understood. Death was the lesser of two evils. My shaking hand gripped the wrought iron rail as I descended the stairs. My inner child wept for the life I could have had, and the life I'd have to live.

Midway down the staircase, Sergei lifted his head. His stone cold expression gave nothing away. His onyx eyes took me in from head to toe as if he was taking inventory.

At the bottom of the staircase, I stood and waited for the formal introduction. My father walked to me. With his hand at my back, he pushed me forward. In my four-inch heels, I stumbled and would have fallen to the unforgiving floor if Sergei hadn't gripped my elbow to steady me.

"This is Katya, your fiancée." His words sounded harsh like a dog's rabid bark.

I wanted to tell Sergei if he turned around and left right now, he'd be able to avoid the marriage, but I knew the man in front of me wasn't here for me. I looked around the house—a mansion, really. Over twelve thousand square feet of pretentious luxury. No, Sergei was here for this. I was simply the price of entry.

He leaned in and kissed my cheek. "Ti takaya krasivaya."

"Thank you." Though his words said I was beautiful, nothing warmed the ice in his eyes.

"In my house, we speak Russian," my father warned me.

Sergei wrapped his arm around my shoulders and pulled me to his side. "My future bride is wise to speak English. We are in America, are we not?" He looked at my father. "Yuri, you speak what you want, but Katya and I will speak English."

If I weren't so afraid of getting my face slapped, I would have laughed. Here was a man who came to be my father's second in command, but he acted like he was the king and my father the pawn.

In perfect English, my fiancé said, "Let's get better acquainted, shall we?" He turned from my father and walked me out the front door. I waited for my father to say something about Sergei's disrespect. We hadn't been given permission to leave, but only silence followed us.

Once we were down the stairs and safely on the path leading to the pool and the gardens, I asked, "Do you think it's wise to poke the bear?"

"What does this poke the bear mean?"

"You might not want to antagonize my father. He's not a nice man."

Sergei laughed. "You think I am?" He raised a brow—a perfectly groomed brow. Odd for a man who probably ate small children for breakfast, and devoured teenagers for lunch. "I'm not here to make friends with your father."

"You will work for him."

"We'll see." Sergei chuckled. It was a warm rumbling sound that at any other time would have been comforting, but it wasn't. Sergei had an agenda. He came to America for something, but it wasn't to marry me. "Now show me our home."

The way he said "our home" confirmed Sergei would never be anyone's second.

We walked through the gardens to the pool house. While my Manolos looked great on my feet, they weren't designed for long walks. They were sitting shoes. The kind of girl wore when she tucked her feet to the side so the slit in her dress led the eyes from the pair of do-me heels to the lacy edge of her thigh-high stockings.

We took a seat at the umbrella-covered table, and I did just that. I shifted the hem of my purple dress, but Sergei's eyes never left my face. While the side slit showed an obscene amount of skin, he didn't seem to notice, or care. Nope, Sergei had no interest in me.

While I didn't care to marry the man, I wanted him to want me. The art of seduction was my only superpower. If I could get Sergei to want me, I, at least, had some control in my marriage. If not, I might as well jump from the balcony now.

"I believe honesty is the best path forward in a marriage, don't you?" he asked.

While my head nodded, inside I laughed. Honesty got you killed, but so did lying. There was no right answer. The difference came to choice. Honesty would kill you faster. Lying was like a poisonous insect that kept biting until its venom ran so deep inside, you'd never recover.

Never let your right hand know what your left hand is doing, my mother used to say. Living with my father made her the best of liars. Who knew while she smiled and organized my eighth birthday party, she was planning her death?

If Sergei wanted honesty, I'd give it to him; at least my misery would be over quickly when he reached over and snapped my neck.

I sat up ruler straight and steeled my shoulders. I was a Petrenko, and while that didn't say much about my integrity, it said a lot about my strength. A girl couldn't live with a devil for too long and not become strong. "I don't want to marry you."

He raised his hand. I prepared for the blow, but instead, he cupped my cheek and smiled at me. "Nor do I, you." He looked me up and down. "While you are attractive, you are not my type."

"Why marry me at all?"

He dropped his hand and sat back in the seat. He appeared not to have a worry in the world. "It gets me closer to the prize."

In front of me was a sprawling estate. A resort style pool—waterfall included. It was over the top. Add valet parking and a doorman, and no one would be able to say this wasn't a five–star hotel. We had a full staff that included everything from a lawn boy to a chef.

"You want this?" I pointed toward the pool, the gardens, and the house. A spiral of smoke rose from the master suite deck. There was no way Yuri Petrenko wasn't watching. "You'll have to kill him first."

Sergei stood and offered me his hand. "Perhaps. I'm leaving my options open." He turned his back to my father and bent over like he'd kiss me, but he didn't. "It would be wise to leave yours open as well."

Love, hate, and loyalty warred within me. Did I tell my father Sergei might kill him? Did he deserve fair warning? None was given to Vincent Wilde before he was shot dead on the sidewalk outside of Old Money Casino. That was how this whole mess started. My father couldn't be happy with what he had. He wanted more, and he went after it without any thought to the consequences.

Thoughts of Old Money brought back memories of Matt. As the middle son of the recently deceased leader of the Italian mob, and the younger brother of the man I was supposed to marry, he was the first person to help me without expectation. Soon I'd have to tell him the truth. He spent three years in prison because I put him there.

"Where did you go in your head, little one?" Sergei brushed a wisp of hair from my face. How funny that his soft touch would no doubt be able to crush my skull with a single squeeze.

"Just wondering what my life will become. What's expected of me in this marriage?"

We walked toward the house. "You will give me a son. After that, I don't care what you do. Just be discreet."

His words stopped me. "You would allow me a lover?"

"Give me what I want, and I will give you the world."

"What if I wanted your heart?" I didn't. I could never love a man like Sergei. His focus was on money and power. Love was like a unicorn.

Everyone searched for it, but it often remained elusive.

"The only way you'll get my heart is if you carve it out with that knife strapped to your thigh."

I ran my hand along the skirt of my dress. "How did you know?"

"It was a guess, but it pleases me."

Did it please him that I protected myself or that I felt I had to? "Trust doesn't come easy for me."

"It shouldn't." He pressed his lips to my forehead. "Trust no one."

"Not even you?"

"Especially not me."

I can't say he didn't warn me. Sergei Volkov was clear about his intentions. He came here to win. When it was all said and done, he'd have it all. He'd own this house, own the Petrenko businesses, and he'd own me.

There was nothing I could do about any of it except take a header off the balcony, but I wasn't my mother, and I refused to be so weak as to let a man decide for me. There had to be a way out of this. I'd figure it out if it was the last thing I did.

On the cobblestones beneath my father's balcony, Sergei turned to me. "We will work out the details, but for now let's seal it with a kiss."

Dread raced through me. How I thought I'd get through a marriage to a man they called the Bull, I had no idea. When I looked up and saw my father looking at us with hate in his eyes, I decided to give him the show he expected. He created this situation, and we'd both have to deal with the consequences. There was the devil I knew on the balcony, and the devil I was supposed to marry. At this point, I had no idea who would be worse.

Sergei's lips pressed against mine. The kiss was all wrong. There was no passion. There was no desire, but I faked it because that's what I did best. I opened my mouth to him. When his tongue touched mine, I held back the bile that rose to my throat. My eyes closed, and I pictured Matt Wilde. This would be our first passionate encounter, and he wasn't present. I wondered as I deepened the kiss and ran my hands up my fiancé's back to his crew cut hair if he knew in my mind I wasn't kissing him. Sergei's lips were merely a convenience. In my head and in my heart, Matt was with me.

CHAPTER TWO

You can take the man out of the mob, but in the end, he'll always be a mobster. Sitting in my father's leather chair, I looked around his office—my office, and wondered if I'd ever be able to be legit.

Vincent Wilde was an asshole. He beat his kids, abused his wife, and took whatever he wanted, when he wanted. That made him a bad man in everyone's eyes. He was my father, and that gave him a margin of latitude in mine. Without him, I wouldn't be here sitting in his chair running a multimillion-dollar hotel and casino.

Love and respect were different things. I

didn't love my father, but he had demanded my respect. How was I supposed to overlook his murder? We were taught that every action had a reaction. Every decision had a consequence. Someone had to pay for my father's murder. I rubbed the scar just below my right ribcage. It would be a constant reminder of how Yuri Petrenko wielded too much power.

I kicked back in the soft leather cocoon and watched the monitors on the wall. Fifteen screens that switched every few minutes from table games to slots to the bars, clubs, and restaurants in Old Money Casino.

A soft tap on the door drew my attention.

"Come in." I sat up, straightened my tie, and smoothed the lapels of my new jacket. I'd come a long way in a few weeks. Gone were the prison orange bags and the hospital gown that showed my ass. In their place was a custom tailored suit.

"I'm going down to the coffee shop in the lobby. Do you want anything?" Mrs. Price asked.

"Surprise me." I hadn't had a decent cup of coffee in years.

"If I brought you nothing, that would be a surprise," she teased.

"But you'll bring me something because you

came in here to ask, which means either you're simply doing your job or you're being extra nice because you want a raise."

"Fetching coffee isn't my job. As for a raise, I'll never turn down well-deserved compensation, but in this case, I was being considerate." She closed the gap and tugged at the Windsor knot at my neck. "You are seriously out of practice. Do I have to tie them all for you and leave them like nooses hanging in the closet so all you have to do is put it on and give it a tug?" Which was what she did right, then.

"Would you?" I got my answer with a slap to the side of my head. Mrs. Price was more than an administrative assistant. She was family. "Hey, don't forget you work for me."

She laughed. "Keep telling yourself that. Even your father believed that bunch of malarkey." She turned and walked to the door. "Don't get yourself into trouble while I'm away."

I wondered if she saw the glint in my eyes that said retribution was coming.

"I should manage to stay out of jail while you're gone."

She left, and I opened my new laptop. My fingers floated across the keyboard like they recognized it as home. I was rusty, but it wouldn't take me long to get my skill set back. I'd need to hone my craft to get back at Yuri. He'd taken so much from me. The bastard took three years of my life when he turned me in to the feds for laundering money—his money. There was no doubt in anyone's mind Yuri was responsible for our father's death. Add to that the hit in prison that nearly killed me, and it was understandable that Yuri Petrenko needed to pay for his crimes.

The keys clicked under my fingertips until the screen blinked, and I couldn't believe what I saw. Had she left her computer unprotected for me? Surely, Katya knew better than to leave a way in. While her skills at hacking weren't as fine-tuned as mine, she did have skill. She'd managed to pilfer hundreds of thousands of dollars from her dad before he noticed. That was the crime that got me on Yuri's radar.

"What are you doing, Katya?" I whispered to no one. I took over her camera and zoomed in. She sat on her bed in a purple dress with her head buried in her hands. When she lifted, lines of mascara marred her face as tears streamed down her cheeks. That wasn't the Katya I knew. The girl I knew would gut you before she allowed you to hurt her. So much had changed while I was gone.

I'd always had a thing for the pretty little blonde; it's why I didn't turn her in to her father when I found out she'd been the one stealing from him. That and the fact that she was supposed to marry my brother. It was a union that would bind the families and end a war between two rival syndicates.

Plan B was what she called her theft. I wasn't sure if the money was to escape her life from Yuri or the marriage to my brother. She never loved Alex, and he didn't love her, but there was no mistaking the chemistry we shared. It sparked like a frayed wire each time we were together. The pull between us grew stronger each time we met. The problem was, there could never be an us because she was a Petrenko and had been my brother's fiancée. That all changed when Alex married Faye and broke the contract.

Still, there was no way we'd ever be more than a tumble in the sheets. She was still a Petrenko, and I was a second son with nothing to offer her father. In our world, we were like two dogs going after the same bone. While we may be able to exist in each other's worlds for short periods of time, eventually one would devour the other.

I stared at the screen for a few minutes, wondering what would bring this woman to tears, and then remembered her statement at lunch the other day. She said she was to marry Sergei Volkov if she couldn't kill him first. Had she done it?

It was a simple enough task if she got close enough. I'd heard she had some serious knife skills. Add to that the fact that she was a Petrenko and undoubtedly lacked an empathy gene, and there was no doubt she could avoid the marriage with the slip of a very sharp blade. Worse case was, she could do like my brother did and marry another. However, that would probably end up with her and her new husband buried six feet under.

I zoomed out and took in her room. There was a big bed and over-the-top old-world furnishings. Was that her style, or was she simply a prisoner in her home?

The door opened, and I closed the computer. No sense in getting caught spying. When I looked up, it wasn't Mrs. Price with coffee, but my brother Alex.

"Want the chair back?" He was the oldest and by all rights should run the family business. The problem was, Alex didn't have a passion for gaming. He liked developing properties. He'd always stayed on the legal side of things. I, on the other hand, loved the seedy side of the business. Gaming is a numbers and fists racket. Both I was good at.

He took a seat in front of the desk. "Just came to see how your first day back is going?" He looked toward the door where Sam leaned against the frame.

As far as bodyguards go, Sam was good. He seemed to know where I was each second of the day. Big like his brother Tony, he was hard to miss. Intimidating as hell, but he somehow stayed quiet and out of the way.

"Glad you took my advice," Alex said

"It's not like you left me much choice. It was hire a goon or have you as a shadow."

"This thing with Yuri isn't over."

It's just begun. "What's the plan for Yuri?" I hoped there was a plan, but deep inside I knew there wouldn't be. Mob life was an all-or-nothing endeavor. You couldn't almost pull the trigger and then get the outcome you wanted.

"No plan. We're out. We need to let the law handle Yuri. Just watch your back."

I slammed my fist on the desk. The cup of pens fell over, and several rolled off the desk to the tile floor. Sam stepped inside the room and evaluated the situation before he stepped back through the door. "You can't let him get away with what he's done. He killed our father. Hell, he almost killed your wife, and he tried to kill me. In my book, that's three, and it means he's out."

Alex took a deep breath and let it out slowly. "Agent Holt is working on it."

"Right, and that's why his son Mikhail is sitting in jail right now instead of Yuri. How long will everyone pay for his crimes? Hell, even his daughter is going to pay the price. Do you know anything about Sergei?" I opened my computer to search for the Russian gangster and stopped cold when I glanced at the screen. Sitting in front of the keyboard was a nearly naked Katya. Maybe it was because I'd spent the last three years in prison, but her small lace covered breasts were perfect. A jolt of awareness rippled through me and landed between my legs. I really needed to get laid and fast.

"Something you want to show me?" My brother lifted to his feet.

I exited the screen and typed in the name Sergei Volkov. No pictures came up, but there was a lot of information about the man. Called the Bull, he had a reputation of pushing his way around. He'd risen in the ranks of the Bratva quickly. It was purported that he was the mastermind behind taking out an entire organization in Dublin, Ireland, all because he considered the Irish inferior. He was the equivalent of the Russian equalizer, except he didn't have Robin Hood tendencies. It was said that what Sergei wanted, he got.

I turned the screen to face my brother. "He's here, and he's after something. Katya is only a piece in the puzzle. She's a way in, but once he's there, what happens to her?"

Alex unbuttoned his jacket and leaned back into the chair. "Do you and Katya have something going on?" His eyes never left the screen, and it made me wonder if somehow I'd managed to bring her room up again, but when I turned the computer back toward me, there was only text.

"No…I mean, I like her as a person, but we've never…" I wasn't the kind of guy who'd sleep with his brother's fiancée.

"But you wouldn't turn her down if she offered?"

I wasn't the blushing type, but heat rose to my face. "I've been in prison for years. A stiff wind sounds appealing. Hell, I'd do Mrs. Price just to empty my sac."

As luck would have it, she walked into the office with my coffee. "I'm flattered, but Mr. Price doesn't share. I can call a service to help you with that problem if you'd like."

I jumped up and rushed to her. "I'm sorry. I'd never want to—"

She held up her hand. "Young man…stop at I'm sorry and live." She turned around and walked out the door.

I spun around to face my brother. "Can I fire her?"

"Sure, but make sure your funeral arrangements are made."

"How did Dad put up with her?"

Alex laughed. "Her? How did she put up with him? There is always the possibility that she was the one who put the hit out on him." My brother joked because we both knew it was Yuri. Hell, even his daughter said so. Mrs. Price wasn't the enemy. She had my best interests at heart. So did Alex, which was why he was here.

"So what do I have to watch out for now that we're legit?"

"Same as before, except now you don't get to beat the shit out of card counters. You don't have to worry about the feds breaking into the secret, high-stakes games. You don't have to cover the trail of tax evasion and illegal liquor sales. No beatdowns for extortion. No payoffs. No hits. No jail time. Keep it clean." He gave me the Wilde eye, the one that said he'd be happy to take Dad's bamboo cane to my ass if I stepped over the line.

One thing I learned in prison was to look innocent. While my mind was finding a hundred ways to screw the system, my Boy Scout good looks never gave me away.

"Straight and narrow as an arrow," I said. "You don't have to worry about me."

Alex looked at me for a long minute. "What about Katya?"

"We'll send her a fruit basket on her wedding day," I replied without emotion even though my gut twisted to know she would have to marry that monster.

"Good to hear." Alex rose from his chair. "I'm meeting Faye at Gatsby's for lunch. Do you want to join us?"

I looked to monitor fifteen, which showed Gatsby's Bar, where Faye sat in the booth across from her friend Trish. "No, you go ahead." I raised my cup of coffee. "I'll stick with this for now. I've got stuff to catch up on." I rose and walked him to the door.

"Remember what I said. Yuri will be dealt with." He gave me a bro hug and left.

Yes, Yuri would be dealt with. There were two ways to deal with a man like Yuri. Kill him outright or make him suffer. I always believed that Karma was a bitch, and right now my name was Karma.

I tapped a few keys and brought Katya's room back into view. Gone were the perfect pair of breasts, and in their place was nothing but an empty space.

"I'm coming for you, Yuri."

I went to work doing what I did best—hacking. Katya had left a path open. For me, it was like inviting me inside her home. It would be rude not to accept the invitation. She only made it easy to get to her computer, but that led me to their security system. It only took me two hours to work my way into the firewall and another hour before I had access to everything. The asshole hadn't changed much since I'd been there three years before, or maybe he had and Katya was throwing me a bone by reverting it back to what it used to be.

I had no idea the game she was playing, but games were more fun when played with others. When it came to this game, I was going all in. I'd throw down my chips and see where they lay. I might not be able to touch Yuri physically, but I could do a lot of damage from where I sat.

I hadn't planned much for my post-incarceration life. I had two goals to achieve. The first was to get Katya in my bed at least once. The second was to kill Yuri, but not before he suffered.

CHAPTER THREE

Dressed in torn jeans and a T-shirt, I made my way downstairs for breakfast. I took my meal alone at the table by the window. I always seemed to be alone, now, more so than ever before. I envied families like the Wildes, who despite their differences, enjoyed meals together. Last Sunday, they invited me to dinner. I'm sure it wasn't because they liked me but because I'd saved Faye's life. In the process, I'd ruined my own.

Getting to Alex and Faye's house was tricky. It wasn't easy to escape my father. Telling him I was getting a massage to ease my menstrual cramps did the trick. When it came to men, all a girl needed to mention was her period, and they asked no questions. He would have killed me if he'd known I was having dinner with his rivals and a federal agent. No one discussed business that day except for me. I couldn't hold back the despair of being freed from one marriage, only to be promised to another. My marriage to Sergei couldn't be considered anything but a business transaction.

In the distance, two blue jays fought over a twig. Just like people, they battled over worthless things.

My stomach twisted, sending acid to my throat. I swallowed and kept it down like everything else in my life. While I knew I'd end up married to Sergei, I couldn't erase the uneasiness that came with our first conversation. There was no doubt in my mind he was sent from Russia to eliminate my father, but why keep me? Why not take both of us out? Surely, he could fake a home invasion, kill us both and take over the territory. What was I missing?

Angry voices echoed in the silence. My father's bellowed over Sergei, shouting, "I will not."

Hope sprang from my heart that he'd come to his senses and realized I was not a tradable commodity. Against my better judgment, I snuck down the corridor toward my father's office and stood out of sight.

"You have no choice but to loosen the reins," Sergei said. "I will be taking over the liquor sales since you lost control. Profits are down. We need the Wildes back on board. Leave it to me, and I will make it happen."

"That will never happen. You'd have to kill him and take over his territory."

"Perhaps. I'm leaving my options open."

Fear twisted inside my gut. Sergei was not beyond killing anyone to get what he wanted. I'd never allow Matt to die over cheap vodka.

"This is my territory, and I decide what happens," Yuri yelled back. "I agreed to give you my daughter and make you my son-in-law, but I will not turn over everything to you, and I will not allow you to tell me what to do. Who do you think you are?"

"I'm the man who will change your life. The only thing you get to decide is if it's for better or worse."

"We'll see about that," my father said.

The thunk of boots grew louder and closer. Fear of getting caught forced me to race back to the kitchen and take my seat by the window. A moment later, a shadow loomed over me as I stared up into the coal-black eyes of my future husband.

"You don't have to sneak around, my love. I am an open book."

How the hell did he know I was there? "I…I didn't want to interrupt."

"How much do you know of your father's business?" The chair scraped across the tile floor. The wood frame creaked when he took a seat. Sergei had to be at least two hundred and fifty pounds of pure muscle and brawn. It was a wonder the spindled legs of the chair didn't collapse beneath him.

I considered his question for a moment. Was he testing me? Did he want to know if I snuck around corners to spy all the time?

"I fear my answer may get me in trouble."

He leaned forward, setting his hand over mine. His one palm completely covered both of my hands. "There is no right or wrong. There is only the truth, and the truth is never wrong and always right."

"You realize you are contradicting yourself."

He smiled. "I know exactly what I'm doing, my love."

How he tossed that term of endearment around so easily bothered me. Love was something special, or it should be. I'd never known the emotion myself, except for the way a daughter loves her mother. "You do not love me, so please refrain from calling me your love."

His eyes danced with amusement. "My future bride is either bold or stupid. Why do you challenge me?"

"I cannot help myself. Everything is a battle, and I am a warrior."

"Good. I don't have time for soft females. Tell me what you know?"

Though I didn't want to give away family secrets, wasn't it my father who had given me to this man? If he were going to be my husband, I'd have to tell him, eventually. Maybe in the process of getting to know him, I could figure a way out of this mess.

I looked toward the hallway where my father was either stewing or plotting a hit on Sergei. "How about I show you instead?"

"Perfect. Get your shoes, and we will meet outside."

When I walked out the front door five minutes later, I was greeted by a group of men I didn't recognize.

Sergei stood by me and pointed to each man individually. "This is my security team. Abram,

Egor, and Timur." All three men nodded in my direction. "You have your own security team?"

Timur opened the door to the black sedan. He stared at me with the same black intensity as Sergei did my father. A chill raced down my spine. He was definitely Sergei's right-hand man, and there would be no hesitation to protect him.

His eyes glanced to my thigh, where my jeans hugged my skin. "Are you armed today?"

I patted my purse. "Of course I am. I'm not stupid."

He slid into the seat beside me. When the door closed, he said, "So you're bold."

I directed the driver to old Las Vegas, where the clubs we owned were located. We pulled into Boodeem. When translated to English, it meant *to your health,* but I was sure the three men killed there this year didn't consider the place a threat to their health until they were on their knees in front of Dima, begging for their lives. Defaulting on debt was unhealthy. Defaulting to the Russian mafia was deadly.

"I have to take care of myself. I have no mother, and you know who my father is. Can you blame me?" We exited the car and walked into the dimly lit bar that smelled like aftershave and cigars. I waved to Mike the bartender, whose eyes grew wide when he saw the men surrounding me.

When he picked up the phone, I shook my head. Something told me a call to my father would be unhealthy for Mike.

"This way." We weaved through tables to the back room, where a single knock opened the door. Sergei pushed his way through. I smiled at the gatekeeper, hoping to convey a message of calm.

Only two tables were in play. The stakes were high with no maximum bet and a minimum of five thousand a hand. These games weren't for the faint of heart or those who were light in the pocket.

"Just gaming here?" Timur asked. He scanned the room like a hunter looking for prey hiding in the dark corners.

"No, there are women upstairs." I'd never been upstairs. The place scared the hell out of me because I knew deep inside I was one argument with my father away from being chained to a stained mattress and sold for some man's pleasure.

"Show me." Did he see the shudder that shook my body? I lifted my chin and walked the men to a back door that led to a single staircase. When we entered the second floor, we were greeted with the smell of cheap perfume and silence.

Sergei pulled me back and took the lead. He opened doors to rooms as he walked down the hallway. Some had women sleeping, but there were no chains. No un-plunged needles in arms. The last room had a couple caught in the act. The man looked over his shoulder as he thrust into the young brunette.

She groaned but didn't seem to mind the intrusion. "Mimi's across the hall, she can take care of you," she said and went back to her task at hand.

While I never wanted to be sold to the sex trade, at least the girls seemed safe.

Sergei rapped on the door across the hall and waited for Mimi. An older woman answered. "Fifty bucks for a blowie, a hundred for full-on sex. You want a creampuff, that's double." She adjusted her shirt so her breasts nearly toppled out.

"Just introducing myself. I'm Sergei, your new boss."

"Right. No cash—no coochie, mister."

She tried to close the door, but I stepped from behind Sergei. When the woman saw me, her face turned ashen.

"Mimi, is it? Let me introduce you to my fiancé." It pained me to say the words. "He'll be taking over for my father, Yuri. I suggest you treat him well." My greatest hope was that Mimi was Sergei's type. If he could find his pleasure from a woman like her, I'd be off the hook.

"So sorry." She knocked on the wall in a pattern, and half a dozen women opened their doors. "Girls, we have special guests."

While Timur and Sergei passed on the offerings, the other two men disappeared with waiting women. As we exited, the hallway was no longer silent, but filled with the sounds of sex.

"Shall we have a drink while we wait?" I asked as we walked by the tables and entered the bar.

"I don't wait," Sergei said. "We'll continue. My men will catch up. I'd like to see the warehouse."

Talk about a punch to the gut. I'd promised myself never to set foot in that building again. I still had nightmares of the moment I buried Dima's knife inside his stomach.

Contrary to popular belief, my reputation for being able to kill without thought was propagated by me. If people were afraid, they wouldn't mess with me. My bravado was nothing more than a good concealer to hide my weakness and imperfections.

"There's nothing but crates of liquor at the

warehouse." I kept moving toward the front door, hoping he'd change his mind.

"It's where my cousin Dima died, and I would like to go there."

I stumbled at his words and fell to my knees. Quickly, I tugged at my shoelace and pretended it was the reason for my fall. I took in two silent cleansing breaths before I stood. "Dima was your cousin?" A jump from the second-story balcony was looking better each day. I pulled out my best performance. "I'm so sorry for your loss. I had no idea. Dima never talked about family."

Timur yanked the car door open, and we slid inside.

"Do you know anything about his death? I'm told it was the Wildes who killed him."

Could he see my heart pound against my chest? "No, I know nothing about that day, only that he was taken by surprise."

For the first time since I met him, Sergei showed his anger. "That's a lie," he yelled. "My cousin was perfect at his job. He'd never be taken by surprise. Did you know they cut off his balls before they slit his throat?"

I moved to the corner without thought, trying to gain distance. I couldn't feel too bad that he lost his penis. He was a sick bastard. The real question was, did that injury kill him, or had I delivered the fatal wound when I had stabbed him?

"Why do you cower?" He narrowed his eyes until only slivers of onyx showed. "It's not like you killed him, but I will find out who did. My cousin isn't the only one with skills. Tell me about the Wildes."

My mind was still on skills. Did it turn him on to torture his victims? Was I not his type because I wasn't bleeding or begging for my life?

"Oh, I don't know much about them."

"You were engaged to the oldest. How can you not know them?"

I couldn't stop the eye roll before it happened. "I'm engaged to you, and I don't know anything about you."

He nodded his head and looked out the window. "I'd like to pay a visit to the brothers. I hear they own a club called Capone's."

"I don't know if an unsolicited visit is wise."

Sergei reached over and gripped my jaw. The strength of his touch was guaranteed to leave a bruise. "I didn't ask for your advice. I merely need answers."

As we neared the warehouse, my throat tightened and my heart raced. "Of course not. Yes,

Capone's is a nightclub. I'd be happy to take you there tonight."

He pulled back, dropping his hand. "Perfect. We can celebrate our engagement."

Timur opened the door. Sergei hopped out. They stared at the warehouse entrance. "I assume you can get inside."

I glanced at the door. Had it only been weeks since I was here? It felt like years ago and yesterday at the same time. I shimmied my way across the seat and stood on shaky legs. This was a do-or-die moment. One thing Sergei had already proven was, he didn't miss a thing. Which meant he'd see my fear if I didn't get a handle on things. It was time to put on my game face.

"Even if I didn't have the code, I'd be able to hack into the system easily enough. It's a simple program." I wanted to slap my hand over my mouth. My hacking skills were something I'd kept on the down low. A back pocket skill I'd used to my advantage more than once.

Sergei laughed. "That's good to know. I'm in need of a good hacker."

The only reason to need a hacker was to spy or steal, and something told me he intended to do both.

"I didn't say I was good." At the door, I entered

the code, and the lock sprung free. Even though the warehouse reeked like wet wood and whiskey, I still smelled the iron-tinged scent of death.

Timur and Sergei walked around the storeroom and stopped at the exact spot where I'd left his cousin to die. *How did he know?* I ventured a step forward and saw the dark stain inked into the concrete.

Timur's hand came to rest on Sergei's shoulder.

When Sergei turned to face me, I saw the vein in the center of his forehead pulse and the look of pure evil wash over his face. Blood would spill over Dima's death. Hopefully, it wouldn't be the Wildes or mine.

"It could have been anyone. Even the Colombians are jockeying for position."

"Nyet," Sergei snapped.

"This is your father's fault. He will pay."

I backed to the doorway. This was my fault, and I should pay, but before Sergei could wrap his hand around my neck and squeeze, I needed to tell Matt his family was in trouble. Until then, I'd play dumb.

"My father didn't kill Dima. He loved your cousin."

Sergei stalked toward me. "Your father didn't pull the trigger, but he loaded the gun when he killed Vincent Wilde."

How could I convince him that wasn't true without giving myself away? "The Wildes would never kill Dima."

"Not even to save Faye?"

Shit. I forgot my father's part in kidnapping Faye. "What does Faye have to do with this?" I asked as if this was new information.

He cupped my cheek in the way a lover would. His soft touch was in direct opposition to his cold stare. "You don't know much, do you, my love?"

I knew more than I let on, but that was my secret to keep.

CHAPTER FOUR

At five o'clock, my computer screen flashed big red letters that said WARNING over and over again. When I hit the return key to dismiss the obvious prank, an upside down Italian flag replaced the cautionary message.

The intercom button rang, the buzz replaced by Mrs. Price's voice. "I'm leaving," she said.

I pushed button number one and responded, "Have a great night." My attention went back to the computer monitor. I'd left a door open to my computer in case Katya wanted to walk in and play games with me, but this was more than a game. She knew better than to throw out a distress signal. In our world, no one cried wolf unless the beast was ready to take its first bite.

I stared at the flag for minutes, trying to decipher the message. Was she in trouble? I seriously doubted that. The woman was like a polished iron fist. She was pretty to look at but deadly if she hit you.

"What's your game, sweetheart?" I pushed the button on the bookcase behind my chair and waited for the wall to shift to display a fully stocked bar. With the bottle of Beluga Vodka and a glass in my hand, I returned to my computer and stared at the flag on my screen.

The first shot of vodka went down rough, but the second was smooth. Turns out I liked more than Russian women.

As I thought about the sassy blonde with the perfect breasts, I considered her message. Katya was Russian. If she were in danger, surely she would have sent the Russian flag upside down. Instead, she sent the Italian flag. It was a warning to me.

I picked up the phone and called Alex. He answered on the second ring.

"What's up?"

I leaned in to the screen to make sure nothing was hidden between the red, white and green stripes.

"I think Katya sent me a message—a warning."

As I sat back, I smiled. I was a true Italian through and through because I knew the flag was upside down at first glance. The stripes were backward with the red stripe first, which was wrong.

"What do you mean?"

I told Alex what I'd received. "Stay away from the Petrenkos. She's warning you for a reason. In fact, stay away from Katya."

A growl escaped. "How can you not want to help her? She saved your wife?"

Alex sighed loudly. "It's not that I don't want to help her, but there's no way to help her without declaring war with the Russians. We no longer have the manpower to survive. I'll call Agent Holt and tell him something is going down."

It was funny that my brother still called his father-in-law Agent Holt. After a family dinner Sunday night with him, Katya, and the others, I had to accept that Michael Holt wasn't a bad man. He was just doing his job when he arrested me.

"Fine," I said in resignation. Alex was right. He'd shut down the "family business" and turned us legit in a matter of months. I owed him to try to keep it that way.

"You promised, Matt. You said you'd walk the

straight and narrow. There's no way we all survive if you don't."

The truth was a razor-sharp blade to my heart. While turning my back on Katya felt wrong, disrespecting my brother's wishes was worse. Katya wasn't family. Alex and my baby brother Rafe were all I had left in the world.

I pressed escape, and the flag disappeared along with thoughts of the petite blonde with the big attitude.

Sam walked inside. "You want dinner, Boss?" While I sat drinking vodka, poor Sam was starving to death.

"Sure, I can order room service unless you want to take a break and head down to the cafeteria."

"I could stretch my legs if you think you'll be okay while I'm gone."

I pulled my gun from the top drawer. Funny how I was supposed to toe the line, and the first thing my brother handed me when I got to his house was a weapon. He knew it was illegal for an ex-felon to carry a firearm, but I suppose he weighed the risk against the reward. In this case, being able to protect myself was a fine reward. We may be out of the mob business, but that didn't stop others from wanting what we had.

"I'll be okay. I'm going to finish up here and then head back to the apartment. Stella is making pasta if you want to join me there."

Sam gave me a look that said it all. He was an employee, not a friend.

I closed the bar, picked up my computer and walked down the corridor to my new apartment. Hard to believe Dad was gone. Harder yet to believe I was in charge of Old Money Casino. With the flash of a keycard, I walked inside my new home. The air smelled like garlic and fresh bread.

Stella rushed from the kitchen wearing an apron that said, "Kiss the Cook", so I did. A big, wet one on her cheek.

She rambled in Italian. I was rusty with the language after spending years in a cell with a guy who only spoke English—and not well. But I got the gist of what she was saying. It was something about making all my favorite foods.

She led me to the dining room table designed for twenty and set for one. There was no way I'd sit at the massive table and eat by myself, so I picked up the plate and headed for the tiny café table in the kitchen.

"You should eat in the dining room. It's where you belong." She stirred the pasta sauce on the stove.

“I don’t want to eat alone.” I glanced at the table she’d set for herself and placed my silverware and plate across from hers. “You’re family and we eat together.”

The corners of her mouth lifted into a smile. “Go change. I remember how you eat, and that shirt is too nice to ruin.”

“Thanks for your confidence. You know I’m nearly thirty, right?” I tugged at the tie Mrs. Price had to fix this morning.

“You know I helped raise you, right?” she countered. “Now get out while I finish dinner.” She brandished a spoon covered in red sauce and chased me out of the kitchen.

My first few nights of freedom were spent at Alex’s house. Tonight was the first night I’d spend alone. With a few minutes to spare, I walked through the apartment. It was silly to call it that since it took up an entire wing of the floor. With at least a dozen bedrooms, a library, office, gym and sauna, it was bigger than most houses in Vegas.

Of the three of us, I probably spent the most time here. Dad wasn’t really social. If you were invited to his home, it was because he had something for you to do or you were in trouble. I’d spent plenty of time on both ends of that equation.

In the living room decorated in old-world charm, I moved to the window that looked over the strip. It was in this exact place I stood when Dad told me he'd agreed to a marriage between Katya and Alex. That was the day I hated him the most.

While I'd never dated Katya, I'd crushed on her since we were little. Despite our families being at war with one another, we often ended up in the same social settings, so we learned to get along. The first time she walked into a party wearing a red dress and heels, I was a goner. I was twenty-one, and she was sixteen—too young to approach, but sexy enough to admire from a distance. Over the years, each time I entered a place I knew she'd be, she was the first person I sought in the crowd. Just over three years ago, in this same spot, my father said that once Alex and Katya were married, the two families would work together. That's the day he sent me over to Yuri's to find out who was stealing from the Russian mobster. Also the day I realized it was Katya.

Yuri knew I could track the person down to a splice of DNA if I had to, so when I refused to tell him who had pilfered his cash, he set me up and turned me in. That was the beginning of the end or maybe it was the beginning of the beginning because everything changed.

Walking into the master bedroom felt surreal. It was the king's lair. Decorated in dark, rich colors, it spoke of wealth and power. While it wasn't the same as when Dad was here, I still felt his presence, only he was no longer the king. I was.

Ten minutes later, dressed in jeans and a black T-shirt to hide the pasta sauce I would spill on myself, I joined Stella for spaghetti and meatballs.

"I miss Faye," she said.

"You see her all the time." I twirled spaghetti on my fork and shoved the big bite into my mouth.

Stella gave me a dirty look. "Don't tell me you lost your manners in that horrid place."

I nearly choked. I might be rounding thirty, but Stella made me feel like a kid. "Sorry." I hung my head. "It's so good though."

"It looks like I won't be missing Faye too much if I have to retrain you."

"You love having someone to care for, and you know it." Stella had been around longer than I had. She'd served the Wildes her whole life. "Maybe you should get a boyfriend."

She yanked at the hair curling by my collar.

"Maybe I should get the soap for your mouth. I don't need a man. I have my boys." She smiled with the pride of a mother. "But I liked having a woman around. I liked having a daughter to spoil." She smiled wide. "You'll have to bring me one."

I laughed around my partially chewed garlic bread, which not only got me a scowl but a yank to the ear.

"Don't hold your breath. There are no women on my radar." *Except Katya.* Only she was off limits.

"I won't hold my breath, but I won't give up hope that the right woman will land in your lap."

I finished my dinner, and despite Stella's complaints, I helped her clean the kitchen. She headed to her quarters while I walked to Dad's office with my computer. Something was off with Katya, and although I wasn't supposed to get involved, nothing said I couldn't snoop.

On the wall in front of the desk hung fifteen monitors. It was the same system in the office. Dad liked to have his eyes on everything. Too bad Yuri wasn't as smart. While Katya let me in the door, it was his lack of firewalls that let me into his accounts. The money he amassed was significant. Yuri was doing okay for himself these days.

With the touch of a button, I could make it disappear, but what was the fun in that?

I scrolled through his expenses. He loved his tailor, his masseuse, and the escort service he spent thousands on weekly. It gave me a chuckle that he had to pay someone for sex. Most men with his kind of money got it free. Hell, the man ran his own brothels, and he still had to pay.

While I was in his accounts, it made sense to me to make sure Yuri gave back to the community he took from. I set up automatic payments to several charities. Money would go to Alcoholics Anonymous, the Human Trafficking Fund, and the Widows of Warriors Fund. It was the least I could do with Yuri's money. I made sure the amounts were enough to make a difference, but not so much that it would alert anyone. It simply looked like Yuri was being philanthropic.

I heard my mother's voice in my head say; *Don't expect anyone to do something you wouldn't do yourself.*

I went into the Old Money Casino accounts. While we weren't in the financial shape that Yuri was since we became a legitimate enterprise, we weren't hurting for cash. I transferred a large sum of money to Gambler's Anonymous.

Feeling like I'd accomplished something, I

leaned back and kicked my feet up on the desk. The screens in front of me changed every few minutes. It was like watching a video game where a lot passed me by unnoticed. Then a flash of red caught my attention.

My feet dropped to the floor, and I rushed to the screen that held an image of Capone's. Staring straight at the monitor was Katya, surrounded by four fierce looking Bratva soldiers.

CHAPTER FIVE

I was the meat in the middle. The single slice of turkey shoved between an entire loaf of bread. Flanked on both sides, I disappeared into the booth.

Had Matt gotten my message? My hope was he did and he'd stay away.

The little redheaded waitress bounced over. The fringe of her dress shook long after she stopped moving.

"What's it gonna be?" She stared at Sergei as if she knew he was in charge. He had an air about him that people picked up at first glance. He was not a man to mess with.

Sergei looked at me. "A bottle of Crystal for her and a bottle of vodka for the men."

The woman, whose name was Kris, eyed the group. "Reverse harem? Lucky girl."

Bad luck was the first thought that entered my mind.

"Nice place," Sergei said. "I'd like to own it someday."

A bubble of laughter slipped from my lips.

"You find that funny?" How was it that sometimes his voice didn't give a hint to his heritage, and sometimes, like now, it was laced with an icy accent and infused with intimidation?

Immediately, I shook my head. "Not so much funny as an impossible goal. This property has belonged to the Wildes since it was built." I had to talk past Timur since he sat between Sergei and me. It was like leaning around a freeway pylon.

"Nothing is impossible." The waitress arrived with both bottles. She quickly made work of popping the cork and pouring me a glass, which I drank straight down and refilled. She left the vodka and shot glasses for Sergei. He poured them all a drink and raised his glass in a toast. It was a toast I'd heard many times. Family first. Death before dishonor. In the end, only one man can win. Be that man.

They tossed the shots back and poured another round. Before anyone could offer a second toast, a shadow fell across the table. All four men grew before my eyes. I quickly poured my third glass of champagne and stared at Matteo Wilde. My heart raced at seeing him again. Matt didn't need a suit to define him. He pulled off badass in torn jeans and a T-shirt just fine.

He raised his hand to the waitress, who rushed over. "This is shit. Our guests deserve better." He took the bottle of Stoli Gold and handed it back to her. "I didn't expect the Russians to send me a welcome home party."

Not one man moved. They all stared at Sergei for direction. When he placed his hand flat on the table, they relaxed or at least shrunk by an inch.

"It's important to know one's enemies and allies," Sergei said.

Matt leaned against a nearby table. "Which am I?"

No one spoke.

"It's unclear," Sergei finally said.

Kris showed up with five clean shot glasses and a bottle of Beluga. Her hands shook as she poured the drinks.

"Let me," Matt said. He lined the drinks up and upturned the bottle, moving from glass to glass in a single move. He set one in front of every man at the table before he looked at me. "Katya, would you like a shot?"

I shook my head. Half drunk on three glasses of champagne, I didn't need to add hard liquor to the mix.

"Let's toast to bountiful business and beautiful women." Matt raised his glass. His eyes never left mine. "I hear you are to be married."

"News travels quickly," Sergei commented.

Matt smiled. "You are in the town that never sleeps."

Sergei reached past Timur and placed his hand over mine. "Yes, Katya and I will be married on June 21st."

Had someone sucked the oxygen from the room? My hand went to my throat as my airway closed and threatened to suffocate me.

"No," I said without thinking. All eyes turned to me. If looks were fire and I was wax, I'd have already melted into the velvet upholstery.

"No?" Sergei lifted a brow.

I reached for my inner warrior. "Are you sure it was June 21st? My father hadn't mentioned a date."

He lifted his hand to my chin. A quick reminder of how painful his touch could be. "The date is up to us, and I chose that day. Is there a problem?"

Emotions choked me. I pulled in several deep breaths to get the spots dancing before my eyes to disappear. This wasn't a time to show weakness.

"No, that day is perfect." When I looked at Matt, he was scowling.

"Of course your fiancé would know, but this is a tough month for the Petrenkos. If my memory serves me correctly, Katya's mother passed away in June."

How he remembered, I couldn't say. Funerals and weddings were the only time families lowered their guards and weapons. Matt was just a boy when my mother died. He'd come to the funeral dressed in a suit. It was the first time I'd seen him dressed up. His presence was the nicest thing about that day because he was the only one who smiled at me and told me things would be okay. It was a complete lie. Things were never okay, but in that moment I believed him.

"I'm sorry, my love," Sergei said and dropped his hand, "what day did your mother kill herself?"

It was in these times that I knew Sergei Volkov was an evil man. He could have asked the day she died, but he had to remind me that my mother had taken her own life. He didn't pour salt on a wound. He sliced me open and doused me in rubbing alcohol.

"June 21st," I whispered.

"Perfect. We shall erase the bad memory and bring in some good."

I smiled. It was all I could do. All I was allowed to do. "Excuse me." I lifted my champagne glass. "I've had too much to drink and need the ladies room."

Sergei shifted out of the booth first, followed by Timur, then me. As I walked away, I felt ten sets of eyes on me. The last thing I heard before I turned the corner was Sergei telling Matt they had unfinished business.

I rushed to the bathroom. At the sink, I stared into the mirror at the woman I'd become. "I am a Petrenko," I told myself. "I do not quake in fear. I do not cry, and I do not pine for what will never be mine." *Strong words for a weak girl.* Not too long ago, I stood with Faye in a bathroom not too far away from this one when she shook from fear. She'd just married Alex and realized what she'd married into—the mafia.

"I had no choice." The girl in the mirror looked back with steel-blue eyes. Did choice really matter? All I could hope for was a man who treated me kindly. Love didn't exist. What people thought was love was only lust gone wild. No one married for love. Not my mother. Not my father. Not me. If something blossomed between two people, they could consider themselves fortunate. I let out an exasperated sigh.

I would stand beside Sergei and say I do and hope for the best. Maybe he was right. Maybe burying that awful day with a different memory would help. It would either lessen the pain, or it would cover it with something equally horrific. I feared it would be the latter.

After a splash of water to my face and a touch up of bright red lipstick to give me some color back, I walked out of the restroom ready to face the rest of the night.

As soon as I cleared the door, a hand wrapped around my waist and pulled me into a nearby stairwell. My first instinct was to fight, but the man who had me pulled against his chest wasn't there to harm me. It was Matt.

"Are you okay?"

As much as I wanted to stay right there in his arms, I knew I shouldn't. Knew I couldn't. I had minutes before someone would look for me. Or maybe not. That would mean Sergei cared, and he didn't. I had something he wanted, and it sure wasn't what was between my legs.

"Of course I'm okay. I'm a Petrenko."

Matt pushed me to the wall, trapping me on both sides with his hands. "You don't have to wear your armor around me. I watched you cry yesterday."

So he had found the door I left ajar. "Back to stalking?"

"It's not safe to let me in."

"When was safe ever a factor in our lives?"

"Thanks for the warning." He leaned in and took a deep breath.

"What good did it do if you didn't stay away?" I wanted to lay my head against his chest. To feel his arms around me for the very first and last time, but I stood still, trapped between him and the wall. "Sergei is after your family. He thinks one of you killed his cousin Dima."

"Dima killed himself."

I lowered my head. "I killed Dima. I buried the knife in his gut. There was so much blood." A tear collected in my eye. One tear was all I'd allow that asshole.

Matt moved his hands along the wall so they cupped my cheeks. For a moment, I stared at his lips and hoped he'd kiss me. Just one kiss to make me forget everything. A single kiss that could last me a lifetime. "Listen to me," he said, pulling me from my thoughts about his lips and kisses. "Dima killed himself."

"Right." All my sarcasm needed was a roll of the eye to confirm my disbelief.

He pressed his forehead to mine. "Have you been carrying the guilt of his death with you these last few weeks?"

"I don't feel guilty. I feel..." Did I dare let my guard down? Could I trust Matt with my feelings? "I'm scared."

"Sweetheart, you did not kill Dima." He thumbed the tear away. "One of Alex's men cut off his nut sack and threw his knife to the ground beside it. With three of them present, Dima couldn't fight back. He took one look at his neutered self and realized he'd never get off by torturing people again. His life wasn't worth living. He picked up the knife and slit his own throat."

"Really?"

"Really. You have nothing to feel guilty about. Dima killed himself. It's all in the coroner's report." That information was golden because if somehow I could get that report, I could prove to Sergei the Wildes were not responsible, and I wouldn't have to implicate myself. A ripple of joy rushed through me. Before I considered my actions, I stood on my tiptoes and pressed my lips to Matt's. He stilled for a second, then wrapped his hands behind my head to close the gap and deepen the kiss.

His lips were full and soft, not hard like Sergei's, and when he opened his mouth, I tasted the sweetness of cinnamon mixed with vodka. His tongue dipped inside, the velvety softness of it exploring the surface of mine.

When my legs grew weak, I wrapped my arms around his neck. My fingers found their way to his soft curls. For the first time in a lifetime, my heart filled with something other than dread. I knew it wasn't love, but lust on fire. Fire being the important word because I was playing with it by kissing Matt when a contingency of Bratva soldiers was beyond the door.

I pulled away and licked the moisture from my lips. I'd savor his taste forever. Could one amazing kiss last me a lifetime? It had to.

"Don't go." He leaned his body into me. His arousal pressed against my belly.

"I have to, or they will kill us both."

He stepped back and pressed his hand to where he'd been stabbed in prison. "They tried to kill me once. I know Yuri is your father, but he has a lot to answer for. He killed my father. He tried to kill me. Hell, he sent to me to damn prison."

That was another reason to walk away. Matt needed to know the truth, and I needed to tell him.

"There's something you need to know."

On the other side of the door, a man spoke Russian, and the reality of getting caught hit us both. Neither of us was prepared to fight a battle tonight.

"There's no time. Go down one floor and come up the elevator. If anyone asks where you've been, tell them you had to use the casino bathroom because this one was out of order." He nudged me to the stairs. "This isn't over, Katya."

I hurried down a flight and looked up to see him dragging a mop bucket and caution sign from the closet next to where we kissed.

"Yes, it is. At least this kiss was better than the first one we shared."

"What are you talking about?"

I ran down the next flight without giving him an answer.

Several minutes later, I was in the elevator like Matt suggested. The doors opened to reveal Sergei and his men. They had come to look for me.

"Where have you been?" The fabric-covered walls absorbed Sergei's anger. I stepped out and felt draped in fury.

I pointed to the caution sign in front of the bathroom door and the out of order sign taped above it. *Thank you, Matt.*

"I had to go all the way across the casino." I stared down at my heels. "These aren't designed for long walks."

His stiff demeanor softened. If Matt had been around, I would have kissed him again because he saved my ass once more.

"Let's go home," Sergei said. "You have a wedding to plan."

CHAPTER SIX

Was it her kiss or the fact that I hadn't been kissed in three years? Any sane person would have come out of prison and landed between a set of willing thighs, but not me. Nope, I had to get straight to work. Alex didn't have time to run the casino and his development company too. My little brother was packing up his apartment in Boston after finishing his law degree at Harvard. All he needed to do now was pass the bar exam and come home.

"You want a coffee?" Mrs. Price peeked her head inside my office.

"Yes, surprise me." I pulled a ten from my pocket, and she waved me off.

"You own the shop." The click of her heels faded.

My mind went back to Katya and the kiss. Lips that tasted of honey and champagne made the kiss that much sweeter. With the way her tongue made love to mine, I could only imagine what her body could do. I got hard thinking about it. One thought of my brother's warning gave me a softie. I had to respect his wishes to stay away. Katya Petrenko was my kryptonite, but I'd be damned if I didn't want her anyway.

I opened my laptop and virtually snuck inside her room. Had she slept last night, or were her thoughts on that one damn perfect kiss—a kiss that erased the memory of all kisses before it? Did she touch herself while she thought of me like I had her? Did she find her release behind closed eyes and the cloak of a dark room, where she could pretend anything was possible? Or did she climb into bed beside that damn monster? And what the hell did she mean last night's kiss was better than the first one? Unless I was missing chunks of time from my memory, I'd never kissed the woman before. I would have remembered.

On the screen in front of me was nothing but an empty unmade bed with the right side of the comforter crumpled and the left side of the bed smooth and pristine. At least one question was answered. Katya had slept alone.

"Boss?" Sam poked his head inside the door. "Sorry to bother you, but there's a woman here to see you."

"Tell her to make an appointment with Mrs. Price when she gets back." I wasn't in the mood to deal with anyone just yet. To focus on something else would mean I'd have to let the memory of that kiss leave my mind, and I wasn't ready to let it go.

Sam closed the door behind him. Minutes later, he knocked and opened it again. "She says it's urgent."

I slammed my computer shut, pushed away from the desk and stomped to the door. What the hell could be so urgent? When I flung the door open, there stood Katya.

"I got this," I told Sam and quickly ushered Katya into my office before locking the door and pressing her against it. "What are you doing here? Did you come here for more?" I leaned forward and breathed in her scent. Everything about her spoke to me, or at least to my dick. I pushed my hips into hers to let her know how much she affected me. "I was just thinking about you."

Her hands lay flat against my chest. She didn't push me away. She lifted and twisted her neck to give me access, and I took it. My lips brushed along the milky white column. Goosebumps rose as I trailed my tongue from her collarbone to the shell of her ear.

"Why are you here, Katya?" I sucked in her lobe and nibbled at the soft skin.

"I needed to see you. I need—"

"I know what you need." I covered her mouth with mine. Just like last night, I got lost in the kiss. Every cell in my body was on alert. Not the kind of alert that warned of danger, but the kind of alert that told me I was screwed because danger was in front of me and I refused to heed the warning.

The kiss started off demanding and desperate and settled into soft and sensuous. When her hands left my chest to wrap around my back, I knew she was all in. When they traveled down to my ass, I let my hands explore her body. Every delicious curve felt like lightning under my fingertips, and every spark of electricity hit me between my legs.

I grabbed her ass and lifted. She immediately wrapped her legs around my waist. I was exactly where I wanted to be—right between Katya's thighs. Too bad her jeans and my slacks separated us. In this position, I could have slid right home.

Like a teen on his first date, I ground into her, trying to find some satisfaction in our proximity, but the friction wasn't enough.

"I want you," she whispered. "Once, just once, I want to know what it would feel like to have you inside me."

She had me at I, but when the words *you inside me* came out, I was already on my way to the leather sofa. I laid her down on the butter soft surface and stood back to take her in. She was so damn beautiful. A warrior dressed in an angel's body. How could I turn down what she offered? No sane man could.

"You sure about this?"

She pulled off her shirt, leaving only the white lacy bra underneath. Her pert nipples poked against the delicate fabric and begged for the heat of my mouth. I covered one and sucked it through the lace. The moan that broke free from her spurred me on.

"Is this what you came for?" I bit down gently and listened for that little mewl of pleasure I was certain I'd hear. She didn't disappoint me when that sexy, deep sound echoed through the air.

"No, this is not what I came for, but I want it

anyway." She reached for my pants and fumbled with my belt. Her deft little fingers had it loose in seconds. She unzipped my slacks and set my length free. The heat of her palm wrapped around me and stroked my shaft. Nothing ever felt so good.

I pulled the cups of her bra down and took turns suckling perfect pink nipples. My lips grazed her skin, leaving a trail of wet between her breasts and down her flat stomach, where I met the barrier of her jeans. Her hand left me and went straight for her zipper.

I stood and kicked off my shoes before I let my pants fall to the floor. When I looked back at Katya, she was naked on my couch with her legs open and arms wide. I'd gone to heaven.

I gripped my shaft and stroked it slowly while she watched. "You want this?"

Her hips rose as if somehow she could meet me halfway. "Yes. Just once."

I chuckled. "You think once will be enough?"

Sadness crossed her expression. "It will have to be."

I climbed between her welcoming thighs and pressed inside her velvet-like glove. She quivered around me. I closed my eyes and willed myself to not erupt like a twelve-year-old watching his first porn. Buried deep inside her, I stilled and let myself acclimate to her heat and the fist-tight grip she had on me.

"Oh, God," she moaned. Her hips lifted, urging me to move.

"So good, Katya. So damn good." I tested out slow motions and built myself up to a pounding pace when someone banged on the door. "Come back later. I'm busy." I never lost my rhythm.

"I've got your coffee," Mrs. Price answered.

"Later," I shouted as I kept up my pace. When Katya's moans got louder, I covered her mouth with mine. While the kiss was perfect, what was happening between our bodies was so much better. There was a point of no return for a man, and I'd thought I'd reached it several times. Maybe I knew this would never happen again. My body understood this was all it would get of this sexy woman. How I kept up, I had no idea, but the ebb and flow of my arousal kept me hard and inside her.

When she gripped my hips and pulled me tight, I knew she was close. I changed my position to one that would bring her the most friction and pleasure. Seconds later, she exploded beneath me. Not once in all the times I'd had sex had I felt anything so powerful as Katya's muscles milking me to climax. My final thrust took me over the edge, and I poured my heat inside her. None of this was wise, especially the no condom part, but it felt right. Like somehow this one time was supposed to be perfect.

Sweaty and spent, I collapsed on top of her. When she wheezed from my weight, I flipped us over and held her body close to mine.

"Can we stay like this for a moment?" she asked. Her head moved across my chest until she found a comfortable spot to the side of my tie.

"I've got you." The truth was, she had me from the minute I sank inside her body. We'd always had this connection. We felt it in the air when we were together. We arced off each other's current our whole lives. Sparks that ignited each time we came into contact with each other. Today wasn't an accident. It was inevitable. The next problem was what we would do with the truth. Katya and I were made for each other.

My fingers traced the soft skin of her curves from the globes of her perfect ass to the dip between her shoulder blades.

"Why didn't we do this years ago?" Her breath floated across my chest.

"Because you were engaged to my brother."

She lifted her head and stared at me with

soul-piercing blue eyes. “But now I’m engaged to Sergei.”

Her words hit me like a hammer to the chest. The pain crushing the passion we shared to bits. “But you don’t love him.”

She pushed up and straddled my thighs. “No. I don’t believe in love.”

“No? Such a skeptic for someone so young.” I ran a finger across her nipple and watched it pucker under my touch. “You should be able to choose your husband. Why do you allow your father to decide?” Here was the question of the day. Why did Yuri give his daughter to a man who brought nothing to the marriage?

She leaned back so my hand could no longer tease arousal from her breasts. “I am a woman. In my family, that means my worthiness is connected to my marriage.”

“Why Sergei?”

She scooted off me and grabbed for her clothes, but I caught her hand and pulled her back to my chest.

“It’s a punishment. I’m not sure if it’s my father's or mine. I don’t think Sergei was his choice. I think it was the Bratvas' doing.”

My head swam with options, and only one came to mind. “They are going to kill your father to gain power over his assets." Saying it out loud only confirmed it in my mind. "Your dad will be dead the night of your wedding. With Mikhail in jail, there's only you left to run things. The marriage is to get access to your father's holdings."

She squirmed in my hands, but I wasn't ready to let go. Finally, she gave up and relaxed in my arms. "I have no choice. What happens to me and my father is about *his* choices."

"That's a big sacrifice."

She laughed. "It's not beyond him. He has tried to sacrifice me twice. The first time to your brother, and now to the Bull. My father loves the business, but he never loved me."

It was my turn to chuckle. "Not true. Remember the pony party you had for your seventh birthday?" Her father had brought in a dozen Shetlands for her party. What I remembered was how her mother screamed when they ate her roses.

"It all changed when my mother died. One minute she was planning my birthday party, and the next she was dead. After that, my father acted like he hated me. Like somehow I was the reason for everything awful in his life."

I pressed my lips to the top of her head. "I'm

sorry, Katya. I forgot your mom died right before your birthday."

"It's old news, but can you believe I haven't celebrated since? Not a cake or a card or a present?"

I sat up, forcing her to sit with me. Her legs sat on each side of my thighs, and my erection probed her for entrance. She moved until the head slipped inside, and she sighed. "This is what I give myself in advance of my birthday." This time, the pace and pressure were determined by her. She gave, and I took. She took, and I gave her every inch I had. Bouncing on my shaft, she grabbed my hand and pressed my thumb to the exact place she needed friction. I stroked and rubbed. Her breaths came jagged and edgy. She bit her lips closed and rocked on top of me until she found the release she sought. When her insides fluttered against me, I jumped off the cliff with her. She swayed gently as if to get every last good feeling owed to her.

When we caught our breaths, she looked down at me. Softness not normally found on Katya's face emerged. She lifted my shirt and traced the border of my scar. "I'm sorry this happened to you."

I covered her hand. "It wasn't your fault."

She frowned and climbed off my body. While I lay naked on the sofa, she hurried to dress. "Yes, it was my fault."

I swung my feet to the floor and reached for my pants. While I pulled them up, I said, "This was your father's fault. He sent me to prison. He had me stabbed." Her face had gone pale. "I hate that you have to marry Sergei, but if he kills your father, I won't hate it too bad."

Katya slipped on her shoes and walked to the other side of the room. "I need to tell you something."

I finished dressing and went to the bookshelf and opened the bar. I poured us each a shot of top-shelf vodka.

"Is this where you tell me you seduced me to get my child inside of you? How the best way to get back at your father is to put a Wilde in the mix to inherit?"

She looked appalled. "No, although no one would have to kill my father, he'd die from heart failure if a Wilde stood to inherit his kingdom. Besides, if I carried your child, he'd kill me to get rid of us both."

Something feral rose up inside of me. "If you were carrying my child, I wouldn't let him near you."

Her hand went to her stomach. "I'm not carrying your child. You're safe."

I offered her a drink, and she moved close enough to take it, then moved back to safety across the room. Whatever she was going to tell me required distance.

"What the hell do you want to tell me that requires this space between us?" I pointed between her and me.

She brought the shot to her lips and tipped it back. A shudder raced down her body. "You are angry at my father for things he didn't do."

I emptied my glass and slammed it on the desk. "Now you're protecting him. He's whoring you out. You owe him no loyalty."

Her head fell forward. "I just whored myself out to you because after what I tell you, you'll never want to be with me again. You think marrying Sergei is the worst thing that will happen to me?"

I tried to rise, but she held out her hand and shook her head. "Remember our kiss last night?"

"It's my second favorite memory with you, but nothing will top today. By the way, why did you tell me it was our second kiss?"

She took in a long, deep breath that seemed to straighten her spine and pull back her shoulders.

"Sergei kissed me to seal our arrangement. I didn't want his lips on me, so I closed my eyes and pretended they were yours." Her eyes glassed over, and a tear ran down her cheek. She swiped at it and continued.

"Come here and let me kiss you again."

She shook her head. "I can't because when I touch you, I realize how much I'll be missing for the rest of my life. So, I'm going to make this easy for both of us. I'm going to tell you something that will make you hate me, and then I'm going to leave."

I know my expression showed my confusion. My forehead ached with the pressure from my scowl.

"I got through prison thinking about you. I felt guilty each day I pictured you when I pleasured myself. You were supposed to be my brother's wife. Nothing could make me hate you more than I hated myself."

She took a step forward but rocked back to her place against the wall. I'd give her the space she thought she needed until she was finished. Then I'd kiss the hell out of her so she'd remember what we shared until I could figure out a way to free her from her engagement. I glanced down at her hand. The bastard hadn't even put a ring on her finger. That would have been the first thing I'd done.

"Go on," I said. "Try to make me hate you."

Her lips moved, but nothing came out. Her hand brushed through her hair. Long strands fell over her eyes when she looked down to the ground.

"I called the feds. It was me who sent you to prison."

Before I knew it, I was out of my chair and had Katya pinned to the wall with my hand around her throat. Not hard enough to choke her, but enough to send the message that I could strangle the life out of her if I wanted.

The floor fell out from under me. Everything I knew about that day was a lie. All the anger I harbored and the revenge I planned was misplaced. While I still hated Yuri and held him responsible for my father's death, I hated his daughter more. "You ruined my damn life."

She pushed my hand away and sucked in a breath. "I saved your life."

I looked at the beautiful woman who rocked my world minutes ago and destroyed it seconds later. For years, her memory had soothed my pains and sorrows. I'd survived prison knowing I'd saved her from her father's wrath. When Alex came to visit and told me he wasn't marrying Katya, my hopes buoyed that maybe there could be some chance for us.

I was no longer in the game, and she wanted out, but knowing she put me in the position to get me killed was unforgivable.

I unlocked the door and swung it open. "I'm saving yours because if you don't leave now, I might kill you myself."

She raced past me. A stunned Mrs. Price picked up the coffee she'd brought me and shoved it into my chest. It splashed my shirt, leaving a stain over my heart.

CHAPTER SEVEN

Stupid, stupid, stupid. What the hell was I thinking? Somewhere in my head, I thought he'd understand. All I got out was *I sent you to prison* before his face turned to stone.

Fine, I didn't need him. I got exactly what I wanted, which was a moment in time to remember so when Sergei worked on getting a son, I could close my eyes and feel something different. Pretend it was someone else. Something told me I'd have to dig deep to make my body believe that what I felt would be Matt. Just the memory of him inside me gave me a shudder of pleasure despite the hurt that spread through me.

As I walked through the casino to valet parking, my heart grew heavier with each step. I reminded myself that love didn't exist. If it did, I would never survive. How could I when the thought of not seeing Matt hurt so much already?

I waited for the kid who probably just got his driver's license to bring my Mustang forward. The red convertible was hard to miss, its growl sounding out the frustration I couldn't. I hopped inside and took off without thought to anyone around me. Entering the strip without a glance, I nearly collided with a delivery truck that would have no doubt killed the driver and probably me.

I raced at twice the speed limit toward home. What did it matter whether I died? No one would care either way. Sergei might be the only one because he stood to lose something if I were gone.

My father might rejoice. My brother wouldn't care one way or the other. He hated me because our mother loved me. It wasn't that she loved him less. She loved him differently. Being so much like our father, he was a constant reminder of the man she'd learned to loathe.

I'd never given it much thought before today. Too young to understand the dynamics of the mafia, I had no idea if my mother was a pawn as well. Had she been given to my father as some kind of reward, or maybe a punishment? Had her father pissed someone off and was forced to sacrifice his daughter?

In hindsight, it made sense for her to jump from the window. Two things became clear. She was miserable. Death was her best option.

Maybe her death was a learning point for me. Would it be better to marry Sergei and suffer or run upstairs and take a header into the rose garden? As the daughter of a Russian mobster, killing myself was the only thing I could control.

I pulled up to the front of our compound and waited for the security gate to open. The hinges creaked as it slowly swung forward. How funny that I had to wait to enter my prison. It was right then I decided I didn't want to live like this anymore. I'd had one moment with Matt—one perfect moment. Our bodies came together. He stopped being a Wilde. I stopped being a Petrenko. We were just two people finding the joy of being together. An ache in my chest gripped my heart. And the reality of what happened on the couch in Matt's office hit me.

I hadn't only had sex with him. I'd made love to him. There was no other reason for such pain to be in my heart. I'd fallen in love with Matt Wilde the day he saved me from my father. Now that he'd tossed me aside, there was no reason to continue my life of lies.

I pulled my car into the end stall of the garage. Even the servant's spaces were closer. It was a visual reminder of how I stacked up in the household. Dead last. Dead was the keyword.

In the entry, Darya moved the feather duster across the iron rails of the staircase as I rushed past her.

"Good afternoon, Katya."

"Is it?" I rushed to my room and shut the door. I wanted to crawl into bed and bury myself under the duvet, but I'd lose my courage to do what was necessary if I didn't act now. Tomorrow held nothing for me. It would be another day like today, minus Matt. It would be unbearable.

I picked up my laptop and scrubbed all the data from it. I left it open so if Matt decided to come for a visit, all he'd see was a room as empty as my soul. I looked around at the things I had. There was nothing of importance that needed to be dealt with. Clothes and shoes had no value. The only things I cherished were memories of my mother, but those were gone too. My father made sure every hint of her was removed from the house. Everything but the last ribbon she'd put in my hair. I reached between the mattresses and pulled out the silky red strip. Frayed and worn, it had spent many nights wrapped around my hand as I cried for her.

I tied it to my wrist as a symbol of our bond. She was with me at birth, and she'd be with me at death.

I laid out the dress I hoped they'd bury me in and walked out of my room for the last time. I snuck across the hallway to my mother's quarters. As a child, I never considered it odd that my parents had separate rooms, but now it made sense. She'd done her job. She'd given him a son. I'd been a bonus child—a spare not given an ounce of care from Yuri. I was almost twenty-five, and a quarter of a century was enough for me.

I pulled the key from the flowerpot, slid it into the lock, and walked inside. I didn't bother to close the door. Deep down, I wanted someone to come in and beg me not to do it, but I knew no one would. I opened the sliding glass door that led to the balcony.

Mom's roses were in full bloom, their sweet smell filling the air. I leaned over the edge. A rush of adrenaline pushed through my veins. The increased blood flow made my head spin. I could hear my heart in my ears. I climbed on top of the cement banister and let my legs dangle over the edge.

Between my thumb and finger, I rubbed the ribbon and thought about my mother. "Will you be there waiting for me?" I whispered.

I took a final glance around me. This seemed like the right decision. Love was real, but it was too painful to survive. I sat on the edge of the ledge and leaned forward. I knew once I released my hands, I'd topple off. I prayed it would be quick and painless.

Just as my right hand released, a heart-wrenching scream came from downstairs. The sound was like a wounded animal—the wails a constant sound of anguish, disturbing because I recognized my father's voice as he yelled at God. I looked down at the roses and wondered if I'd done it and only my soul remained to watch the outcome. Was my father mourning me? One pinch to my thigh confirmed I was still here.

At the next ear-piercing cry, I climbed off the rail and ran toward his office. Was he hurt? Had Sergei tried to kill him?

Two steps at a time, I raced down the stairs, where I found him crumbled in a heap on the floor. Sergei sat stoically in a chair by the desk.

I fell to my knees. I didn't like him much, but

he was my father. "What's wrong?" I looked over my shoulder at Sergei. His black eyes masked any emotion.

My father shoved me aside. "Get away from me."

Scrambling back, I fell into Sergei, who pulled me into his lap and wrapped his arms around my waist. "Your brother is dead, my love. He hung himself in his cell." He said the words like he was ordering Chinese take-out. As if it was routine to announce the death of a beloved son.

"What? No. That's not possible. Mikhail would never do that." I pushed and squirmed, trying to get away from his grasp, but Sergei was big and strong, and he wouldn't let go. Tears pooled in my eyes. I imagined I looked like the grieving sister. Heartbroken that her brother was gone, but that wasn't why I cried. My tears were spilled for me. Mikhail had beaten me once again. He'd always come in first in everything. How was I supposed to escape my life and leave my father childless? I'd been considered cold-hearted by many because I didn't show my emotions, but today my heart was frozen. I was stuck in this miserable existence. Not even I could be so cold as to make my awful father lose both his children on the same day.

Damn you, Mikhail. He screwed up everything.

When I stopped fighting, Sergei loosened his hold on me. My father stood and walked behind his desk. If it hadn't been for his red-rimmed eyes, I wouldn't have known he'd been crying.

"This changes everything," he said. He looked at me sitting on Sergei's lap. "You will marry this week. I need an heir, and although you're not good for much else, you can at least give me that."

I'd never thought I could feel lower than dirt. My father had reduced me to the value of my womb. Cinders of disappointment and hurt had burned inside me for a long time, but the winds of his hatred fed it. Those cinders were rising up to become an inferno. I was tired of being nothing.

"We'll bury your brother on Sunday morning, and you will marry on Sunday night."

I hopped off Sergei's lap. "No. That is not the way this is going. I refuse to have my wedding on the same day my brother is buried. If you force me to do that, I'll be the next person you put in the ground because I'll fight you to my death over it."

Sergei's hands gripped my hips, and he pulled me back to his lap. "My love is right. She deserves more than a shared celebration."

I spun around at his use of the word 'celebration' when we were talking about burying Mikhail. A glint of light danced in his darkness. A chill went straight to my bones. While I would never be able to prove it, something told me Sergei tied that noose around my brother's neck and yanked him to the rafters.

"She will do as she's told," my father snapped.

Sergei slammed his fist on the table. "She belongs to me now. She will do as I tell her."

While the men fought over my loyalty, I slipped from Sergei's lap and walked to the door. "I will do as I like," I yelled. I turned to my future husband. "I will not marry you on the day of my brother's funeral, nor will I marry you on the anniversary of my mother's death. However, I will marry you, and I'll give you a son because that's what I was born to do. Once I fulfill my commitments, both of you will leave me alone." I spun around and walked out of the room.

I took the stairs one at a time. There was no hurry to get anywhere. The door to my mother's room was still ajar. I walked inside and looked around. Why it remained locked was a mystery. There was nothing of her inside this room but memories. Tea on the balcony. Bedtime stories while we snuggled together under her floral bedspread. I didn't need a room to keep those memories alive. They lived inside me. They reminded me that once someone had actually loved me.

"Ms.," Darya spoke behind me. "You shouldn't be in here with your father home. He won't be pleased."

I laughed. Despite all the surrounding sadness, I found humor in her words. "Darya, he's never been pleased. Why should he start now?" I walked to the bed. "Where is Sergei staying?"

She lowered her head, and a blush rose to her cheeks. It seemed that all women but me found him appealing. "He's in the south wing with his men."

I ran my hand over the soft blue comforter. "He shall move in here."

"Do you have permission to move him?"

I stalked toward her, and she stepped back. "I don't need permission. I'm a damn Petrenko, and if I want my fiancé moved closer to me, it better happen. Don't think for a moment Sergei won't be ruling this kingdom. You better cater to the new king. Never forget, I'm his queen."

I moved like a violent storm across the hallway and slammed my door. I was tired of being a babbling brook. Fury whirled inside me, turning me into a fierce raging river.

I changed into the dress I'd hoped to be buried in. While my father planned my brother's funeral, I dressed in four-inch heels and a little black dress.

I had a damn wedding to plan, and it was time to go shopping. I'd have the rest of my life to mourn, but today I was celebrating because by not dying, I was reborn. The world better move aside because Katya Petrenko was here to stay, and I'd take no prisoners.

CHAPTER EIGHT

As soon as the word of Mikhail's death got to me, I went straight to my computer and snuck into Katya's room. I felt creepy spying on her, but I wanted to make sure she was okay. Why that was important to me, I didn't understand. The woman had told me she'd placed me in prison. Her excuse…to save my life. Funny how it almost got me killed.

I caught a glimpse of her. Wearing a black dress, she pulled up the hem and straightened her damn thigh-high stockings. My dick twitched in response. I'd been between those thighs today. Hell, given that they hadn't used a condom, I was no doubt still between her thighs in essence, and I liked that thought.

How screwed up was it that I wanted to hate her and love her at the same time? My heart skipped a beat when I thought of love and Katya in the same sentence. Surely, my body had misread sex for real emotion. It had been too long, and Katya had been my first since my release. The wires of my brain were crossed.

My eyes went to her milky white thighs, where she strapped on a blade and dropped the hem of her dress. She hadn't been carrying a weapon when she came to my office—at least not on her body. Had she felt safe here? Did she feel in danger now?

I tracked her on the screen like a hawk tracked it's prey. She moved around the room with swift efficiency, putting herself together and grabbing her bag. She turned to the computer and frowned. The last thing I saw was her give me the finger before she slammed the screen shut.

What did I expect? I'd basically tossed her out on her ass. I never gave her a chance to explain. I hadn't wanted to hear her lies, but what if they weren't lies?

I punched his brother's number in my phone and waited for the call to ring through. I had to come clean about the Katya issue, or it would certainly bite me in the ass. I'd be surprised if Mrs. Price hadn't called my brother the second Katya started moaning.

"I heard," I answered.

"News travels fast. It was just a one-time deal." I thought about the second time when she straddled me and took control. "Okay, it was two times, but all within fifteen minutes or so."

"What the hell are you talking about? I thought you were calling to tell me Mikhail was dead."

"Oh, no, I figured you knew that. I was calling to tell you that I had sex with Katya in the office."

"You what?"

"I fu—"

"I heard what you said. Do you have a death wish? She's promised to the Bull. He'll rip your head from your shoulders."

"I wasn't thinking with that head."

"No shit." The turn signal clicked in the background. "I'm five minutes away. Meet me in Gatsby's."

In a matter of seconds, I went from feeling like the adult owner of a multi-million dollar enterprise to the child caught sneaking a cookie before dinner. I shoved my gun into the waistband of my slacks and covered it with my jacket.

"I'll be back," I told Mrs. Price as I walked by her desk.

"If you're looking for round two, I think a service would be safer," she called after me.

I laughed. "You mean round three, and no I'm good. Meeting Alex at Gatsby's."

Sam stood in front of me at the elevator and waited for it to open. When he deemed it was safe, he stood aside in order for me to enter. How funny that having a bodyguard never seemed odd to me because I'd always had one. My thoughts went to Katya. She'd never been protected. No wonder she felt compelled to strap a blade to her thigh.

Yuri always had Dima. Before prison, Mikhail had Yevgeny. Who did Katya have? No one.

I made my way to the bar and ordered burgers and fries from Randy, the old man working today. Waiting for Alex, I toyed with the idea of reaching out to Katya just to ask if she was okay, but what I really needed to analyze was if I was okay. I had so many conflicting feelings when it came to that woman.

Alex walked in looking calm and relaxed, while inside I was as jittery as a chicken at a slaughterhouse.

Randy slid our plates in front of us and

brought ice tea before he disappeared behind the bar.

"Why Katya?" Alex popped a fry into his mouth and waited for my answer.

"Have you seen her? I can't believe you didn't want a piece of that."

"While she's pretty, she wasn't my type. Add in the fact that her father is an unpredictable asshole and no doubt killed our father and tried to kill my wife, I want nothing to do with that family."

"Might I remind you that your wife is not dead because of Katya?"

Alex chuckled. "So you were thanking her on my behalf one inch at a time?"

"Consider her thanked thoroughly." I picked up my burger and took a bite. It had been too long since I'd had a decent burger. This was almost as good as sex. Actually, it was far off from being as good as sex with Katya, but it was satisfying.

"Might I remind you that Katya is as good as married to Sergei, that her father killed our father, that the plan was to kill me after we had married? Hell, he tried to have you killed in prison." He sipped his tea. "If given enough time, he would have gotten to Rafe too."

While Alex and I were in the thick of things in

Las Vegas, Rafe appeared safe in Boston. The reality was, he wasn't safe anywhere.

"Rafe will be home soon. We can keep an eye on him. Speaking of the hit on me, I found out today that Katya set me up and put me in prison."

"I knew that."

I dropped my burger to my plate, sending fries flying. "You knew she set me up and didn't say anything?"

"I found out at the hospital when she came to see if you were okay. She cares about you."

"Funny way of showing it."

"She heard her father talking about putting a hit on you because you wouldn't tell him who was stealing from him. She told me it had been her and you'd hidden that fact from her father."

The memory of that day still haunted me. She'd taken too much at one time, and it threw up a red flag. "She'd been careless. I didn't want Yuri going after her, so I put the money back and refused to tell him who the account belonged to. I buried the information so it could never be retrieved. She thanked me by sending me to prison."

"You didn't know that. You thought it was Yuri. Hell, we all did until she came clean. That girl had a thing for you, and while her actions don't quite make sense, you can see why she thought putting you in prison would protect you. It got you off the street. If you're honest, you were safe until Dad was murdered."

I hadn't considered much when it came to the details. No one had bothered me in prison. I was the son of Vince Wilde, but the minute he was dead, I was the son of no one. Had I judged Katya too hard?

"You don't need to worry about Katya and me. I pretty much tossed her on her ass the second she told me." Though my burger was delicious, I couldn't take another bite. My stomach twisted and ached. "Why didn't you tell me?"

"She asked me not to, and I owed her." He swiped a fry through the ketchup. "While I'm happy you aren't going after Katya, I do feel bad for her. She's a victim, not an accomplice. Stay away from Sergei."

I pushed my half-eaten meal to the side. "Tell him to stay away from me. He paid me a visit last night. Said he wanted to negotiate a new deal."

"He came here?"

My brother grew before my eyes. He sat up tall and fisted his hands.

"He brought Katya and his goons here on the

premise of celebrating their engagement. She doesn't even have a ring on her finger."

"It's not a love match."

Thinking about Katya in love with Sergei made my stomach burn. Thinking of them in bed made my brain ache. Hadn't she told me she wanted one memory to last the rest of her life? Holy shit. She would think of me when he was pressed inside her. I clenched my fists so tight, my knuckles turned white.

"She's a sacrificial lamb. We have to do something."

Alex ignored my plea. "What did you tell Sergei?"

Did he think I'd side deal my way back into the business? "I told him there was nothing to negotiate."

Alex finished his meal. "He'll keep trying until he's got his liquor sales and money laundering back."

"He can try, but we're legit and plan to stay that way." While I wouldn't jeopardize the business, the opportunity to bury Yuri would appeal to me. I'd never been a trigger-happy man, but I wouldn't hesitate to pull it if Katya's father was in my crosshairs.

Alex's and my phones beeped with incoming

messages. It was Mrs. Price informing us the funeral for Mikhail was in two days. Funny how everything halted for weddings and funerals, including grudges.

"I'll go and represent the family," Alex said.

"No, we will all go and show our unity. Besides, Mikhail's death will make Yuri more dangerous." I wasn't the head of the family, but I needed to see with my eyes that Katya was okay. Her world was crumbling around her. A weaker woman would have taken a gun to her head. Not my Katya. She was solid as a rock.

Why I thought of her as mine was baffling, but in my heart, I knew it was true. How was I supposed to stand aside and watch her marry a man like the Bull? I bet he didn't know her favorite color was red, or that she was allergic to strawberries, or that she liked her coffee with more cream than coffee. Hell, I didn't know why I knew those things, but I did. Katya had been on my radar since her seventh birthday party, where she crowned me her knight and gave me the black pony to ride next to her all white one. I was the darkness, and she was the light.

"Fine, but you'll have to behave." Alex rose and left while I sat at the table by myself. Behave wasn't a word that resonated in my brain. If I were going to behave, I'd have to leave her alone. I couldn't, so I texted her.

I heard about Mikhail. Is there anything I can do for you?

Several minutes later, scrolling dots danced across the screen. She was texting back, which gave me hope that I hadn't completely ruined our shaky friendship. I stared at the screen, waiting and waiting. The dots stopped, and there was nothing. She was done with me. I couldn't blame her. I'd acted impulsively. I'd responded without all the facts. She had indeed chosen me over her father, which said something about her feelings for me.

I'd taken what she offered freely. She'd shown up this morning and put it all on the line. She'd given me her body. I wondered if she realized she'd taken my heart when she left.

I typed in the two words I owed her. The two words I should have said in person.

I'm sorry.

CHAPTER NINE

Hours passed as I made the necessary arrangements for my wedding. There were some benefits to being Yuri's daughter. When I told the Russian Orthodox priest I needed him three weeks from now, he nodded. When I told him I wanted to marry in front of the Bellagio Fountains, he said no problem. When I asked for the hotel to book an already scheduled ballroom, they didn't blink an eye. I was a Petrenko, and it didn't matter if my father loved or hated me. To disrespect me meant disrespect to him. Any form of insult would not be tolerated.

I amassed hundreds of thousands of dollars in debts in a few hours. If my father wanted me married, he'd foot the damn bill. All my life, I'd been easy. I fell into place as a woman in a crime family. I held no power. I had no control. I did what I was told but no more. Everyone around me had an agenda, so why shouldn't I?

There were too many balls in the air. Juggling wasn't a skill I'd mastered. It was hard to keep everything in perspective when my world was disintegrating around me. Wasn't a big wedding every girl's dream? I'd scheduled mine in the same way someone ordered delivery pizza.

While getting it done was a relief, there was no joy in the event. Nothing made sense. I walked into the little Italian Bistro outside of the Bellagio and asked for a private table. Once my glass of wine was poured and my meal was ordered, I buried my head in my hands and cried. These were the only tears I'd shed for my brother. While he'd always been an asshole, he was still mine. There was a certain amount of loyalty expected when it came to family. At least he protected me as much as he tortured me. That couldn't be said for my father. With Mikhail gone, I was truly alone in the world.

First-time brides weren't supposed to go it alone. Who would help me pick out my dress? It was the last thing I had to do. It was something my mother should have been here for. I was furious at her. How could she leave me?

I stared at my phone. There were two texts from Matt. One to say he heard about Mikhail. Hard to believe he'd feel anything, especially when it concerned my brother. Those two were like oil and water. The second time, he said he was sorry? What was that for? Sorry for screwing me and then kicking me out of his office? Sorry for not listening when I tried to tell him the truth? Sorry because he was an asshole too?

As I sipped my wine, I thought about my mother. Was she sorry as well? Sorry didn't help if it came with nothing. In three weeks I'd be Katya Volkov, no doubt in four weeks I'd be pregnant. Nine months later, I'd be lucky if I weren't dead. Sergei had no need for me except for my womb. He needed the heir to the Petrenko fortune to secure his position.

As if my thoughts summoned him, my phone lit up with an incoming call.

"Hello," I answered sweetly while giving him the finger.

"Where are you?"

"Planning our wedding, my love." Never had I considered or would consider Sergei my love, but he would be my husband, and if I hoped to survive any of this, I'd need to be better at his game than he was. The man was a damn mannequin. He never let his body show what was going on inside his head. I'd be smart to learn that trick.

There was a minute before he replied. "For that, I am pleased."

Which meant I'd disappointed him in something else. "I've got a few more things to iron out. I'll be home then." The word 'then' was nebulous. He couldn't be upset about when I came home if the only reference to time was the word 'then'.

"I'll be here waiting."

Shit. I held up my empty glass to signal the waiter for a refill. Next, I texted Faye. While we weren't close, she was the only female I could call a friend. I did save her life, and for that she owed me.

Where did you get your wedding dress?

It wasn't like I loved her dress, but she managed to get it in hours. I'm sure it was over the top expensive, which was my objective at this point. My father wanted this marriage, and it came with a high price tag.

Couldn't kill him yet?

So she remembered my statement at her house. I'd told everyone at the table that I had to marry Sergei if I couldn't kill him before our wedding day. Since I'd so callously stabbed Dima, no one doubted my ability to pull it off.

No. I'll marry him. It's not like there are others waiting in line. And it's not like I have much choice.

The waiter brought my wine and lasagna and left.

You should have a choice.

I laughed. It wasn't like Faye had much choice either. It was either live in a box on the side of the street or marry Alex. She'd chosen Alex, but I'm sure there were moments when the box looked like it might have been the better option.

For some things, we have no choice. As for my wedding dress, I do.

While I generally didn't eat much, I dug into my plate of lasagna. There was no doubt my life was going to change, and I needed the energy to get through each minute.

I'm not doing anything right now. Meet me at Camille's in an hour? I owe you.

I was glad we were on the same page.

Forty minutes later, I walked into the bridal boutique dressed for a funeral but looking for a wedding dress.

"Can I help you?" The woman took me in the same way a gold digger looks for her next husband. I wasn't a person. The price of my clothes and accessories were cataloged from my Gianvito Rossi shoes to my Gucci purse. I was a commission.

"I'm looking for a wedding dress. Non-traditional."

She gave me a pruned expression. "So you want a cocktail dress?"

"I want something expensive. Something that will make my father gasp when he gets the bill."

Her lips smoothed into a smile. "Do you want him to merely gasp or faint?"

I'd never seen my father faint. "Something that will require CPR please."

The bell above the door rang, and Faye walked inside.

The woman left me and rushed over to her. "Mrs. Wilde, it's lovely to have you back."

I rolled my eyes. "She's with me," I said.

Immediately, we were ushered into a private room.

Faye gave me a hug. "I'm so sorry about your brother."

I swallowed the lump in my throat. "These things happen to families like ours."

"I'm so glad Alex is out of the business."

Laughter bubbled from inside. "You can't believe that's true. You're certainly not stupid, but geez Faye, are you having a moment? You can take the boy out of the mob, but you can't take the mob out of the boy. It runs through his veins."

"No, they're out."

"If you say so, but what happens when my husband comes after yours because he thinks he killed Dima? What happens to your family when my father goes after you or Matt or Rafe or Alex because he swears you are responsible for killing Mikhail? Will you all sit and wait for the bullet, or will you reach inside for your inner Gotti or Capone?"

"Are you telling me something?"

The older woman rolled in a rack of dresses and walked away. I thumbed through them. "Are you listening?" I asked her.

"How do you know?" Faye stood next to me and looked over my shoulder at the dresses.

"I have ears and eyes." I pulled a short dress from the rack. It had a detachable skirt in the back. The price tag said thirty thousand dollars. "Take this dress, for example. It's one-third the cost of a hit."

Faye's mouth dropped open. "It costs ninety thousand dollars to kill someone?" she whispered so the saleswoman didn't hear.

"About a hundred, but I'm rounding up. I recently saw a large withdrawal for waste disposal in my father's account. I can't imagine paying that kind of money to get rid of household rubbish. Can you?"

Faye pressed the short gown with the skirt into my hands. "Try this on. I have to call Alex."

"Maybe you're smarter than I thought." And maybe I wasn't all that bright myself for telling her, but deep inside I cared about the Wildes. While Matt had broken my heart, I didn't hate him. I understood him. After some thought, I could see why he was angry. I'd taken three years of his life away. I'd do it again if I thought it would guarantee he'd live.

I slipped out of the black dress and pulled on the white one. It needed altering. I didn't have the body of a stripper, with big boobs and booty to match. My body was more like refugee meets model. In that way, I took after my mom. How I wish I could see her wedding day photos. Would she be smiling? Was the train of her dress out the door while she stood at the altar like a princess in a fairytale wedding? Did she wear a hefty bag and a belt because she didn't give a shit?

"Oh my God. That looks great on you."

I turned to Faye, who had a tear in her eye. I'd like to believe it was for me, but I was realistic. She was probably scared for her family. She swiped at the tear and rushed forward.

"You think it's okay?"

"You look so beautiful." She laughed. "Much better than me. It was you who told me my ass looked like I'd eaten the seven dwarfs in one sitting."

"I was being childish and cruel. You were stunning. Maybe I'm just jealous that you have an ass." I turned my back to the mirror and lifted up what could only be described as a coattail. "Mine is more like two crackers in a paper sack."

"Matt must love crackers," she replied.

"Matt hates me."

"Give him time. I saw the way he looked at you at dinner. Don't forget, he's new to this world." She pinched in the material, forcing it to hug my breasts. "He needs to acclimate to his new position and being free."

I rubbed my hands down the silk. Even if I

hadn't been forced to marry Sergei, this would have been the dress I'd chosen. It was the perfect mix of tradition and attitude.

"I don't have time to give him." I waved the saleswoman over. "I'll take this if you can alter it quickly. I'm getting married in three weeks."

"Not a problem." She left, and seconds later a tiny old woman shuffled in to mark the dress for alterations.

"I wonder if they have this in red?" I asked. A pin poked my hip even though that wasn't the area the seamstress was working on. I looked down and saw her frown and wondered if my mother would have given me the same look.

"You'll make a beautiful bride in white," the woman said.

When the proposed alterations were pinned, I slipped from the dress. "I'd invite you to be my maid of honor if I didn't think it would get you killed."

Faye handed me my black dress.

"I appreciate that. I would have stood by you proudly, regardless. While I know our families are not going to see eye to eye ever, I appreciate you as a person Katya, and I'm proud to count you as my friend."

Next to making love to Matt that morning,

Faye was the best thing about my day. For a brief moment, everything felt normal.

Once payment was made, I hugged my only friend in the world goodbye and headed for home.

When I arrived, Sergei was waiting in the living room, sitting on the couch next to Timur. Despite the vaulted ceilings and open space, the room shrunk with their mass.

"Is everything set?" He rose and walked to the bar to pour me a glass of Vodka. The thought of needing a drink sent a shiver scurrying down my spine.

"Yes, everything is set but your tuxedo. I assume you have one."

"Of course, my love."

Timur thunked his glass on the table and left the room. There was no doubt he hated me.

"We are ready." At least everything we needed was ready.

"Good." He walked to where I stood and threaded his hand through my hair and yanked my head back. While it didn't hurt, it was a shock. "You do not make the rules for me, do you understand?" He tightened his hold, and I swore I'd be bald on our wedding day if he didn't let go.

"What are you talking about?"

"You had my room moved when I was perfectly happy with my men."

I wrenched myself free. "You are the king and deserve to rule your kingdom. You can't do that by being in the servant's quarters. No doubt my father put you there to show you your position." I knew how to stroke men's egos and piss them off. "If you want respect, find your place."

His eyes narrowed. "You risk much with your mouth."

"I gain much with my marriage. While I'm not your type, I will be your wife, and I will make sure everyone knows who you are."

If at all possible, Sergei grew an inch. "I may keep you after all." He leaned forward and kissed my forehead like he would a sibling. "From now on, you will consult me first." He emptied his glass.

"Of course, my love." Inside my head, I thought, *Like hell, I will.* The worst thing he could do was kill me.

CHAPTER TEN

Alex made a trip to Old Money today to tell me about Faye's visit with Katya last night.

"That girl is still trying to save our ass, and I can't figure out why," Alex said.

I'd given Katya a lot of thought lately. While she was hard on the outside, she was soft on the inside. *Soft and hot and velvety and wet.*

I shook thoughts of sliding inside her body from my head. "Maybe she's hoping we save her." There's always a moment when the truth punches you in the gut. I knew the truth. "She's hoping I save her."

Alex leaned back in the chair in front of the desk. "While I hate to get involved, we do owe her. The problem is, we can't be out of the 'family business' and be in it at the same time."

He was right, but he was wrong. "Don't you want him to pay for killing our father?"

"I do, but not enough to risk my freedom and my life with Faye. Ours may have been a marriage of convenience, but it's been damn good for me. I'm so in love with that woman, I can't breathe without her."

"I get it."

"You do?"

While I'd never admit to being in love, I think a part of me has loved Katya since we were kids. Maybe it was the day she stood by herself at her mother's closed casket that my heart belonged to her. I knew right then she'd be a formidable woman. She stood tall and proud. Though she didn't shed any tears, her lips trembled as she said goodbye before her father yanked her away and sent her out with the maid.

"I know what it's like to love someone. We had a mother."

Alex's features softened. He adored our mother. If it weren't for her, we'd all be in jail. Then again, if it hadn't been for her, we wouldn't be in this position. It was her family that was mob connected. When her father was killed, she inherited Old Money Casino. She married our father and had given him the power he'd always craved. He fell into that category of absolute power corrupts absolutely.

"It's different. When you look into the eyes of the woman you love and see a future that includes children and grandchildren and Christmases and birthdays and anniversaries and you know you'd rather be dead than miss any of that, then you can say you've loved a woman."

"Now you sound like a freaking Hallmark movie."

Alex laughed. "You've watched one?"

"Like I said, we had a mother." The Hallmark Channel played nonstop during the holidays. Mom loved a good mushy love story. She'd swoon when at the end they'd kiss and rush off to their forever. Maybe she watched them to see what the rest of the world experienced because my father was no Hallmark hero.

"Do you think Katya is telling the truth about the hit?" A frown creased my brother's forehead. I always thought of it as his thinking wrinkle, but now I realized it was worry etched on his skin.

I opened my laptop and hoped she hadn't shut me out of her father's accounts like she had her room. A minute later, I was inside. After positioning my computer so Alex could see, I scrolled down the statements and there was an entry for a hundred grand. The payee was listed as number two, which could be anything, but something told me it was code for the second Wilde.

"Do I want to know how you got into Yuri's accounts?"

"No, you don't want to know, but I'll tell you. Katya let me in. Obviously, she wants us to see what's happening."

Alex rubbed the scruff on his jaw. "What if she's setting us up?"

"For what purpose? What does she have to gain?"

"You're right. I bet this has everything to do with Dima. Now I wish I had killed that asshole myself."

Just thinking about him slitting his own throat after being castrated made bile rise to my mouth.

"He's dead, so there's that."

"Yes, but there's no satisfaction in knowing he took his own life. What a coward." Alex rose and went to the bookshelf, where the bar was hidden. He pushed the button and watched the shelves divide and a bar fall into place. "I totally need one of these at the house." He reached into the small refrigerator that Mrs. Price filled each day and took out a soda. "What are we going to do? The hit can be on any one of us. Hell, it could be on Rafe or Stella or even Faye."

I considered the most likely target and knew it would be me. "He's not going to go after you or Faye because you don't have what he still wants. I do. He wants the casino, and while he knows he'll never get it, he'll do what every ignorant, spoiled man-child would do. He'll play the if-I-can't-have-it-then-you-can't-have-it game."

"It still doesn't get him the casino." He took his chair and stared at the bank statements on my computer. He leaned in to get a closer look. "Is he donating to Alcoholics Anonymous?"

A smile crossed my face. "He is now."

"Matt, you're playing with fire. Don't get us all in hot water because you have a grudge to settle."

Anger flared in me like a spouting volcano. I ripped up my shirt to show the jagged red scar where I'd been shanked in prison. "Grudge? This isn't a damn grudge. He's lucky I haven't pulled a damn Scarface and introduced him to my little friend." I yanked the Glock tucked into the back of pants and set it on the desk. "I owe him. I'm respecting your wishes. That's the only reason the news hasn't reported his death."

"Funeral is tomorrow. We should be safe there, but I'm not taking any chances. I'll buff up security and vest yourself."

"I hate those things, they're hot and heavy."

He gave me an I'm-the-head-of-this-family look. "Do it. I'll call Rafe and tell him to be careful. You tell Stella to stay inside."

I wasn't happy about any of it. "Fine. I'll vest up, but I'm not going to cower at some threat from Yuri. For all we know, it's a hit on Sergei."

"Why the hell would he put a hit on Sergei? The Bratva would be on him like stink on shit," Alex commented.

"They are on him, which is why Sergei is here. The business is a mess. His family is falling apart. He's making moves that are putting the whole organization at risk. You don't think they know he killed our father? Tried to kill me? He made the big plays and failed."

"It's a volatile situation."

"What do you think of Sergei?" I asked.

"I don't think anything about him. Whatever he does shouldn't affect us. We're supposed to be out. In fact, we shouldn't even go to the funeral."

I rose from my chair and walked to the window. "Didn't you beat the crap out of Mikhail weeks ago?"

"We beat the hell out of each other. What's your point?"

"We have to go. It would be disrespectful to not show up. Besides, you may not care about Katya, but I feel like we need to be there for her, if not for anyone else. She's been risking her neck for us, and I'm not turning my back on her again. She deserves more. You stay home if you want, but I'm going for Katya."

Alex grumbled. "You're right. It's important to show a united front." He rose from his chair and walked to where I stood by the window. "How are you doing?" He turned his back to the glass and looked around the office.

"I'm figuring it out."

In an uncharacteristic move, Alex pulled me to him and gave me a hug. "I'm proud of you." He dropped his arms. "None of this is easy, but you're doing a great job."

I nodded. "I haven't killed anyone since I got out."

"That's a good start. Let's get through tomorrow, and we'll call it a successful week." He walked to the door. "I need to get home. Faye is making eggplant parmesan."

I'd never seen my brother look so happy and relaxed. "You really do love her, don't you?"

Alex laughed. "I'm so whipped. It's crazy. I'd do anything for Faye. She changed my entire life. Someday you're going to meet a woman who gets under your skin. When that happens, God help you because she will rule your universe."

I looked back outside. Traffic was moving on the strip. The sun was setting, and the lights of the city began to glow. "Then God help me because that woman is Katya. I can't get her out of my head."

"You need to let that one go. Nothing good can come from it. She's marrying Sergei in a few weeks. While I appreciate everything she's done for our family, we can't go to war over her."

I smiled and walked my brother to the door. He wouldn't go to war over her, but I refused to let her be a casualty in whatever game Yuri and Sergei were playing.

I sat in my chair and opened my laptop, hoping she'd let me back in, but she hadn't. I needed to see her. Needed to touch her. Needed to tell her I was sorry. Oh hell, who was I lying to? I needed that woman to be mine.

I had three weeks to figure out a solution. My first thought was to open a bank account in her name and give her enough money to flee. The selfish bastard inside me wouldn't allow it because if she left Las Vegas, she'd leave me, and that wasn't acceptable. There had to be a way we could have it all.

For the next two hours, I made the rounds of the casino. It was important to make sure the employees knew who was in charge. I shook hands and smiled despite my inner turmoil. I walked into my office and looked at my computer. My fingers pushed on the screen, and just before I closed it down, the screen flashed to life and Katya came into focus. I fell into my chair and watched. Dressed in a T-shirt and flannel bottoms, she sat in front of the computer and typed. Seconds later, an email arrived.

Matt,

I got your messages. I don't know what to say, but thank you for giving me a perfect moment to hold on to. I understand why you were so angry. I took something from you. I took your freedom. I took three years of your life. For that, I'm sorry. I thought I was protecting you. I can see now that my actions were impulsive and wrong. Please forgive me.

Yours,

Katya

Damn straight she was mine. I started my

reply when her lips came to the screen. She pressed them to the camera like she was kissing me goodnight, or maybe she was kissing me goodbye. The screen turned black.

"Think again, sweetheart," I said to no one. "You're mine, and I intend to keep you."

CHAPTER ELEVEN

How many times did my father have to look at me and growl? Each time he did, the sound reverberated through the empty funeral parlor. Like always, I was the lamb waiting to be slaughtered. This was the quiet time before the masses would arrive and tell us they were sorry for our loss, but they weren't. It was hard to mourn the loss of a monster. Harder to feel bad for the man who made him.

The director entered and closed the casket at my father's request. It wasn't because Mikhail looked bad but because he looked nice. A sort of calm came over him in death that I never saw in life. I, for one, was grateful because this expression would never leave my mind.

The sweet scent from a thousand fragrant flowers wafted through the air as the doors opened to let the visitors in. It was a smell I remembered well. The smell a seven-year-old girl will never forget because it smelled like lost hope and dashed dreams.

My father pinched my elbow and pulled me to the front of the room, where people would pass by.

My heels clicked across the tile floor as I took up a position beside him. Sergei found his place next to me. I was trapped between two powerful men, both intent on destroying me. My father because he hated me—my fiancé, because it was what he was sent here to do.

I'd given Sergei a lot of thought in the last few days. All you had to do was look at him to realize he'd never be anyone's second in command. The man ate steel for breakfast and spit nails for lunch, and yet, he showed moments of softness when it was needed the most. Most when I almost trusted him, and that made him all the more dangerous.

"Are you okay, my love?" His hand rested for mere seconds on my back before he pulled it away.

I turned my head to look at him. "I'll be fine."

"What a waste," my father said on the end of a breath. "It should have been you."

My internal ember flared, then flickered, then flamed.

"But it wasn't. It was Mikhail. Maybe it should have been you," I whispered back. Out of the corner of my eye, I watched my father's face go from sun-kissed pink, to mottled red, and then purple.

While not smart to talk back to my father at all, it was at least safe to do it here because he wouldn't lift a hand to strike me in front of his peers. To be goaded to violence by a woman would show weakness.

A half-smile was all I had to offer anyone who walked by. While the masses moved through the line and took a seat for the short service to follow, I watched for one man—Matt. My body knew he was here before I saw him. My skin prickled and my heart raced when he entered the room.

God, he was gorgeous dressed in a dark gray suit, crisp white shirt, and charcoal colored tie. While he always looked good, he was a man who could pull off jeans with as much finesse and style as a three-thousand-dollar suit. Why hadn't my father given me to the enemy I knew? Oh, that's right, he did right before he killed their father.

A chill raced down my bare arms. I understood the need to keep a place cold where they stored dead bodies, but did they need to freeze everyone in the process?

As the Wildes grew closer, I got warmer.

Alex Wilde approached first. He looked calm and happy. That's what marrying the right woman did for him. Faye walked beside him. While her eyes were on my father, she kept a serene look on her face. No doubt she remembered the day he had her kidnapped and nearly killed.

On my right, Sergei stiffened and stood taller as the Wildes moved toward him.

Alex stopped in front of me and took my hands. "Katya, is there anything we can do for you?"

There were a hundred things I could think of, but not one that wouldn't start a war. "Thank you for coming."

He smiled and tossed back words I'd said to him the day he married Faye. "For these things, we have no choice."

Next was Faye, who rather than shake my

hand, threw her arms around my neck and hugged me. It was an odd action given the public perception about the hate between our families. "Hang in there."

"By my fingernails," I replied.

She moved on to Sergei, who merely grunted when each person passed, but when it came to Faye, he leaned forward and said, "You are the reason my cousin is dead."

Alex pulled Faye behind him. "You will not talk to my wife. Dima is dead because the coward killed himself."

Sergei lunged forward, but I stepped in-between the two men. "Put your dicks away. This is a funeral. Show some respect for the dead."

Both men pulled at their ties and stepped back into place.

Next was Matt. My father gripped his hand so hard, Matt's fingers turned white, but he didn't flinch. "Yuri, I'm sorry about Mikhail."

Under his breath, my father said, "You killed him, and I will kill you."

Matt stepped back and yanked his hand from my father's grasp. "I had nothing to do with it." He glanced at Sergei. "You should be looking in your own backyard before you try to scale my fence. The Wildes had nothing to do with Mikhail's death. We have nothing to gain. If I wanted to kill a Petrenko, you'd be the first on my list." He moved to his left and stood in front of me.

He held my hands gently. His fingers brushed softly against my knuckles. "You okay?" He leaned in and whispered, "Sweetheart."

"Yes, I'll be okay."

He looked down at my dress, which wasn't black. I'd refused to swath myself in darkness any longer, so I chose an emerald green dress.

"You look beautiful despite the somber circumstances."

"Thank you."

Sergei moved closer. "It's good to see you again, Wilde."

Matt stood nearly as tall as Sergei, but he wasn't as wide. My future husband was large and intimidating, but Matt didn't shrink in his presence.

"Matt, you remember Sergei from Capone's."

Sergei offered his hand, which meant Matt had to drop mine to shake his. He did so, but not before he gave me a reassuring squeeze.

"He's a hard man to forget."

"Have you given my offer much thought?" Sergei asked.

I stared between the two men. *What offer?* I wondered.

"Nope, not even a second of thought." Matt turned back to me and leaned in to kiss my cheek. "Don't shut me out again," he whispered. "I'm going to figure this out."

My breath hitched, and my heart raced. There was nothing to figure out. I would marry Sergei. I'd give my husband a son and my father an heir, and then maybe, just maybe they'd set me free.

Next in line was the Irish contingency. While I had little to do with them, I was familiar with their family. My father hated the Wildes, but he had a special hateful place in his cold heart for the O'Learys. Liam walked past my father without a word and stopped in front of me. "Katya, I'm so sorry about your brother." He held my hand in his the way I imagined a father would when his daughter needed reassurance. I glanced to the man's right and saw his daughter Kirsten. We'd never become friends because of our fathers. It was too hard to separate who we were from what our families did. You couldn't have a sleepover on a Friday night and a shootout the next day. Out of all the mafia families I met, the

O'Learys seemed to be the most family-oriented despite the fact that Kirsten's mother died at her birth.

"Katya, your brother held your hand for a little while, but may he hold your heart forever," Kirsten said.

"Thank you." The Irish were funny that way; they always had something to say, and when they said it, it was like a calming balm to a wounded soul.

Liam held his daughter's hand and walked to Sergei, who turned away from the Irish mobster. Liam shrugged and led his daughter toward a pew. While it was customary to have the service first in most cases, mafia families got the niceties out of the way first in case all hell broke loose later.

I watched the O'Learys walk away. Was it crazy for me to be jealous of the relationship they had? There was no doubt Kirsten would also be used to bring good fortune in marriage, but would she at least have some say in the matter?

The line ended, and we took our seats to listen to the priest say a few words. No one stood to give emotional testimony to the greatness of my brother. He'd terrorized and tortured half the people in the room.

While the priest promised we'd see him in heaven someday, it was simply because he was paid handsomely to put in a good word on behalf of the Petrenko family. None of those words were said for my mother eighteen years ago.

Unlike the Wildes, there would be no celebration of life gathering. We would travel to the cemetery alone and make our way home and back to our normal lives.

After the short service, I stepped into the sunshine. The heat of the rays warmed my skin. At least fifty people gathered on the sidewalk, waiting for the casket to be rolled to the hearse.

Not far away was Matt. He stood to the side and watched me. In a sea of black and gray, I was easy to pick out wearing green.

While I would have loved to feel the comfort of his arms around me, I stayed put and waited for my father.

He led the pallbearers to the hearse, and once my brother was tucked inside, he turned and stomped toward me.

He poked his finger into my chest. "You show such disrespect wearing this color, like the passing of my son is a celebration."

I stepped back from his touch. "I refuse to

wear a color that reminds me of the soulless abyss of your heart."

Yuri leaned in to put his face in mine. "You're just like your mother."

"God, I hope so."

"She was a whore," he spat out. A spray of spittle hit my cheek.

"If I'm a whore, it's not because of my mother; it's because you continue to pimp me out like one."

I'd heard my father talk poorly of my mother on many occasions, but never had he called her a whore. Something inside me reared up like a feral, angry animal. I fisted up and punched him in the nose. He staggered back. When he realized what hit him, he lunged forward and raised his hand to strike me.

I closed my eyes and waited for the hit, but it didn't come. A shadow fell over me, and Sergei stood in front me, holding my father's fist in his hand.

"I'd reconsider if I were you," Sergei said with the threat of death in his voice. "It would be easy to bury two today."

I looked up to Sergei with gratefulness in my expression. That feeling of thankfulness ended quickly when a black Escalade rounded the corner. The window opened a crack, and a hail of bullets sliced through the air. Everyone around me scrambled for cover, but I stood and dared a bullet to hit me. Death was not the worst thing that could happen.

CHAPTER TWELVE

Chaos ensued as bullets rushed through the air. There was nothing more frightening than the sound they made as they split atoms on their way to their intended target. I watched in horror as Yuri hugged the pavement. Sergei was tackled by his bodyguard. Katya stood tall and defiant, as if taunting the gunman or the bullets.

I raced to her aid and folded her in my arms. The impact of the bullet that lodged in the back of my vest sent us both to the ground with her tucked under my body for protection. I reminded myself to thank my brother for insisting I vest up.

The bullets weren't meant for the Wilde or O'Leary families. Each one fired headed straight for Sergei or Katya, and it became clear who Yuri put the hit or—almost clear. My thoughts went straight to Sergei, who was upsetting the balance of power in the Petrenko household. Then again, Yuri could have put the hit on Katya. Without a daughter to marry off, Sergei wouldn't have a reason to stay.

Maybe the hit was on Yuri. If Sergei was intent on taking over the territory, he'd need to get rid of him. All three were possibilities.

When the car screeched away, I moved from Katya. She lay on the sidewalk and laughed. The damn woman laughed.

"What the hell is wrong with you? You could have been killed." I winced at the pain in my back. It was a lot less than had the bullet ripped through my body, but it did feel like I'd been punched in the kidneys with a sledgehammer.

"Nothing is wrong with me."

I rose and helped her to her feet. All around us, people rose from the cement and checked for injuries. No one seemed to be hit. Katya took a step forward and nearly fell again.

"What hurts, sweetheart?" She hobbled to the wall and leaned against it. Pulling up the skirt of her dress, she flinched at the injury to her thigh. The knife she had strapped there had lost its sheath and sliced into her skin.

She smeared the blood aside to get a look at the wound. It wasn't deep, but it was about an inch long. "Dammit. My dress is ruined."

Leave it to a woman to worry about her dress. The blood seeped to the surface and ran down her leg. "Hasn't anyone told you to never bring a knife to a gunfight?" I turned to see who would be coming to look after Katya. As much as I wanted to, it wasn't my place—yet.

What I saw sent fire through my veins. Yuri was at the hearse, talking to the priest as if nothing had happened. Sergei got checked out by his bodyguard. The man was taking inventory of him like he was a sale item on a rack. He turned him around again and again until he was certain he hadn't been hit.

"Let's get you cleaned up." I walked her back into the funeral home.

"Wait up," my brother called after me. "You're hit."

Katya stopped and spun me around. "Oh my God. You're hit." She tore at my jacket until she got it loose. When she didn't see blood, she pulled my shirt from my pants and lifted it to see my vest. "Thank God. I don't know what I would have done if you were injured again."

I looked at my brother, who was flanked by

two of our four bodyguards. "Where's Faye?" I'd grown fond of my sister-in-law and wanted to make sure she was okay.

"I've sent her home with Tony and Frank." Frank was new to our team, but he came highly recommended by Max, who stood with his back to our group, watching for trouble.

"She's probably shaken up. Take Max and go to her. I'll keep Sam, and as soon as I get Katya taken care of, I'll head back to the casino. We should talk."

My brother waited for a few minutes. He looked at Katya, then back to me. "This isn't smart. You know that, right?"

I nodded. "Not smart, but right." I helped Katya down the hallway, where we entered the women's bathroom. I locked the door behind us and lifted her to the counter. She weighed nothing in my arms.

"You should go home. Your brother's right, this is not your place." She leaned over and pulled handfuls of paper towels from the dispenser. She shimmied her dress up to expose what should have been the milky white skin of her thighs. It pained me to see the blood staining her flesh.

I cupped her face. "I'm so sorry, Katya. I should have chased after you the other day. I was torn between who you are and who your family is. You are not your father."

Despite the situation, she giggled. "No, I'd never know what to do with a penis. If I had one, the other day would have looked much different."

"You joke."

She pressed the paper towels against her cut. "If I didn't laugh at my life, I'd never stop crying."

I dropped my hand to where she'd strapped her knife. "You'd be safer with a gun."

Her head fell forward. "My father forbids me to have one." She cleared her throat. "I think he's afraid I'd use it—on him." She gave me a smile that said she'd do exactly that if given the chance.

I pulled the belt free and set her knife aside while I cleaned her wound. With a little pressure, it stopped bleeding. "I don't think you need stitches, but you should put a bandage on it when you get home."

"Right. I'll do that." She fisted her weapon and tried to jump off the counter, but I pressed my body in front of her. Her knees spread to give me room to stand between them.

"I care about you, Katya."

She rolled those big, beautiful blue eyes. "Don't waste your time on me."

I grabbed her shoulders and gave her a shake. "You are a not a waste of time."

"Tell that to my father." She placed a hand on my chest. For a minute, I thought she'd push me back. Instead, her fingers skimmed down my shirt to the bottom button. She worked them loose one by one. "Let me take care of you."

I wasn't sure what that meant. "Here?"

Once my shirt was loose, she worked on the Velcro straps of my bulletproof vest. "I need to know you're okay before I leave you for good."

"I'm fine, and you are not leaving me for good." I grabbed her hands and pulled them to my lips. The hot air of my mouth brushed over her fingers. "We'll figure this out."

"There's nothing to figure out. Someone tried to kill you."

I shook my head. "No. They tried to kill you or Sergei, and my guess would be Sergei. The Bratva sent him, and your father is not happy."

She leaned forward and put her head on my chest. "Maybe they will kill each other and I'll be free of them both."

I stepped back to get a good look at her. "Has he hurt you? Has he forced himself on you?" It gutted me to think she might be sleeping with him.

"No. I'm not his type."

"What the hell does that mean? You're every hot-blooded man's type."

"He isn't interested in me that way. He wants a son. If he lays with me, it will be with that objective in mind."

"He can get a son anywhere. He wants a son with you so he can legitimately inherit the kingdom."

She huffed out a breath. "I'd gladly give him everything if it was mine to give. In exchange, all I'd want is to walk away. I don't want to belong to anyone."

I moved in close so her thighs cradled my hips. I pulled her to the edge of the counter so only the fabric of my pants and her underwear kept us apart. "I'm sorry, sweetheart. You'll never get your wish because you're mine. You belong to me." The thought of having Katya as mine to hold and love forever made my dick hard. I rolled my hips against her sex. That little mewling sound she made had me wishing we weren't in a funeral bathroom but in my apartment, where I'd push her into the mattress and pound that reality into her body.

"I'll never be yours as long as my father breathes."

I unzipped my pants and pulled out my length. She needed to be reminded of what it felt like to have me fill her completely. I pulled the string of her panties aside and thrust deep inside her. "Feel me, Katya."

Her legs wrapped around my thighs, dragging me deeper inside her. "Yes," she whimpered until I moved my mouth over hers to eat up the sounds I knew she'd make when I made her come. When she left this place today, she'd know with certainty that she belonged to me.

"You're mine," I said against her lips. "I'm sorry I lied to myself and I lied to you, but baby, you've been mine forever."

She bit her lips to suppress the moans. I was gentle, but I was thorough. Each thrust into her body was a claiming on its own.

"I'm yours," she whispered. "If only in my heart."

"Screw that. I'll figure out a way to make you mine for good. Trust me."

She nodded. I drove it home and felt her clench around me. She threw her head back as her body ruptured. What started as a flutter became a tight glove milking me to my release. We stayed like that for minutes until we heard sounds in the hallway.

There was a knock on the door. "What?" I asked.

"Mr. Volkov is looking for his fiancée," Sam said.

"Shit," I whispered. I pulled a few Kleenex from the box on the counter and cleaned Katya up before I tucked myself back into my pants. "We're almost finished cleaning her up." I looked back at her and winked.

While she put herself together, I buttoned my shirt and tucked it back into my pants. I walked in front of her to the door but stopped before I turned the bolt. "Don't forget who you are and who you belong to. I will figure a way out soon. Will you be okay?" I hated to leave her in the hands of another, but until I had a solid plan, I had no choice. To claim her today would keep the funeral home busy for weeks.

She pulled her shoulders back and twisted the deadbolt. "Of course, I'm a Petrenko."

She breezed past Sam and walked outside to where Sergei waited with the car. He gave me a look that said he knew exactly what we'd been doing, and I knew he'd use that against me. I waited until she pulled away to exhale.

Funny how in any other situation with bullets flying in a public space, the cops would be all over the place, but add in a few mob families, and no one showed.

They knew we would clean up our own messes. Without a doubt, I was making a big mess of things with Katya.

It fired me up to know she mattered so little to the men who were supposed to take care of her. That was why she needed me.

If I were being honest with myself, I probably needed her more. There was something about her that always managed to calm me from the inside out. It didn't hurt when she calmed me from the outside in. Nothing would ever be as good as pressing into her soft, wet heat.

CHAPTER THIRTEEN

Sergei said nothing to me on the ride to the cemetery. He and Timur looked at each other intently, as if they were privy to some kind of secret code.

"We will watch your father sprinkle dirt on his son, and then we go home. You're a mess, and you smell like Matt Wilde." He raised his nose in the air and breathed deeply. "I hope he wore a condom. I don't want to raise his son."

"Please give me some credit, which is more than I can give you or my father." I pulled the skirt of my dress up my thigh to show the angry gash. "You both left me standing there in the hail of gunfire. It was Matt who protected me." I turned and looked out the window. We had entered the cemetery and were winding around to the Petrenko plot of land. No one was buried there, not even my mother, but there was a large granite stone that had our name on it. Mikhail would be the first to rest beneath it. "How funny that I have to look to our enemy for protection because my family can't manage to care."

We stayed at the cemetery until the casket was lowered and buried, and we headed home. I played with the idea of pitting my father against Sergei. If they were fighting each other, they wouldn't be paying much attention to me.

I turned and faced him. "I want to tell you something, but I feel I'm being disloyal to my father if I do."

He turned and gave me his full attention. "Your loyalty lies with your husband."

"But we aren't married yet."

"It's a certainty, Katya. We don't need love to have an understanding. And I don't need to put a ring on your finger to demand your loyalty."

Wrong. I screamed inside, but I held on to my calm facade because this was a game where I didn't want to find myself on the losing team. "I've been snooping."

His brows lifted. "My intended is a spy? Should I be worried?"

"Not as long as I'm spying for you." I pushed my back against the door and continued. "It's important for you to know about the health of the business." I watched him for some reaction, but of course, there was none. "Let's be honest, you didn't come here to be my father's second in command; you came here to rule. Don't you want to know the value of your kingdom?"

One thing I knew for certain was, Sergei was a big man with a big ego, and the more I fed it, the better. "I'm not a great hacker, but I can get into my father's accounts because he's lazy and cheap when it comes to protection."

"Get to the point. What do I need to know?"

"A large amount of money changed hands recently. I think it had something to do with the attack today. I'm not sure who the target was, but I'd guess it was you or me."

His eyes grew big. "Your father would never be that stupid."

"We are talking about my father. I'd say a hundred grand labeled as waste disposal is telling."

"You keep spying, my love."

"Whatever you need, my love."

Each time I said those words, I wanted to barf, but they seemed to placate him. I needed time to figure this mess out. All I knew was that Matt couldn't be the only one trying to extricate me from this disaster.

We pulled in front of the house, and Timur opened the door to let us out. They walked into the gardens no doubt to discuss the new information I'd given him while I walked inside.

I'd raised my foot to the first step when my father summoned me to his office. While the last person I wanted to see was him, I knew better than to ignore his call.

I kicked off my heels and walked down the hall to find my father sitting behind his desk. It was back to business.

"Sit down."

I did as he told me. I had to pick and choose my battles, and this wasn't one of them.

"What can I do for you, Father?"

He smiled and kicked back in his chair like he hadn't just buried his only son moments before. "How are you?"

My mind drew a blank. Not once in the last two decades had he asked about me. "Given the circumstances, I'm doing well." My fingers ran over the cut on my leg. Though sore, it would heal in a matter of days. "Did you try to have me killed today?"

He laughed. It had been a lifetime since I'd

heard him really laugh. "Silly girl. If I'd tried to kill you, you'd be in the ground next to your mother. That hit was for someone else. Dumb assholes got the target wrong."

"Who?" I sat forward. If the target was wrong, that meant the bullets weren't destined for Sergei or me. "Who did you put a hit on?"

He poured himself a glass of vodka and sipped. He took his time, as if debating how honest he wanted to be.

"I believe in an eye for an eye." He drank deeply and put the glass down. "The Wildes owe me a son."

While I didn't want to give my feelings for Matt away, I couldn't help the gasp that left my mouth. "Matt didn't kill Mikhail. What would he gain from that?"

In a calm that could only be considered clinically scary, he said, "I killed his father, he killed my son."

"You said you believed in an eye for an eye."

My father got up and paced behind his desk. "This is not even. I took an old, worthless man. He took my entire future."

"Matt didn't do that. Alex didn't do it. None of the Wildes are responsible. They're out of the business."

A cackle-like laugh filled the air. "You are so damn dumb. Don't you know? The only way to the leave the business is in a coffin."

"You're looking in the wrong direction." I got up and looked out the door to make sure Sergei wasn't within earshot. "There was no way Mikhail would hang himself. I'd bet my life the Bratva killed my brother."

He walked to the safe hidden behind a picture of the Kremlin. "Your faith and loyalty are misplaced. You're so much like your mother." He dialed in the combination and pulled out a bright blue book. "She got confused, but I sent her out of this world with the truth. Let's hope you're smarter and you don't find yourself in her situation. Don't confuse a good lay with loyalty. One will give you a moment of bliss, the other a lifetime of privilege. Your mother chose poorly and paid the price."

My mouth hung open. Had he just told me he killed my mother? "You killed her?"

"She got what she deserved. Her kind of betrayal could never be forgiven."

I flew out of my chair and ran at him. "How could you kill the mother of your children?" I beat on his chest until he pushed me away.

Standing several feet back, I watched a sinister smile lift his lips.

"You mean the mother of my son." He looked at the book in his hand. "You were never mine." He threw the book at me. The binding grazed my forehead. I reached up to feel the blood oozing from a cut.

"How could you?"

He chuckled. "It was easy enough, one push, and she was gone."

My knees buckled beneath me, and the ground met my ass. "Why didn't you kill us both?"

"A man never bets everything at once. You will marry Sergei and get my ass out of hot water. You'll give him a son. He'll try to kill us both and inherit what's mine, but he won't because I'm older and smarter, and I'm a hell of a lot more devious."

I scrambled to my feet. It dawned on me that they were playing from the same deck. They both wanted the same thing from me. While my father could marry and have another son, it was easier to whore me out, get me pregnant and take my child. I was expendable.

No matter whose plan I fell under, one thing was certain. I had no longevity in either scenario.

I hugged the book to my chest. I recognized it as the journal my mom kept by her bed. I raced away from my father in hopes of discovering the truth.

There wasn't a moment where I'd have guessed I wasn't Yuri's child. I'd been raised as his daughter, but tonight I locked my door and pressed a chair under the doorknob. I'd never felt completely safe in this household, but never had I ever felt in danger. I'd always felt like an outsider. Now I knew why.

Matt asked me to not lock him out, so I opened my computer and let him into my ugly world. If something happened to me, at least there was a chance he would see.

I changed into flannel pants and a T-shirt, then sat in the center of my bed and opened my mother's journal. Why had Yuri kept it when he had destroyed everything else?

January 1st

My New Year's Resolution—never tell the truth. I look at my sweet little girl and wish she could meet her father. I'd considered myself lucky that she looked like me, but now I'm not so sure. We're trapped in this fortress, prisoners of a man who kills for pleasure. I've seen what he's done with our son. I don't want him to erase everything good in Katya with his evil.

I READ through the next few weeks, where my mother talked about me and my brother and how terrible she felt that she'd need to leave Mikhail behind but he was already ruined. She couldn't trust that he wouldn't reach out to Yuri.

JANUARY 15TH

MY PLAN IS SET in motion. He'll ruin her if I stay. I've managed to squirrel money away through shopping and returns. It doesn't amount to much in our world, but a few thousand dollars will at least get us to another city. I've been thinking about new names. Something decidedly American will be best if we want to disappear. Katya will become Katherine, and I will become Anna instead of Anya. When I close my eyes, I see a better world for us. I hope someday Lucky can be a part of it. I love that man so much. For now, I can't risk his life too. How was it I fell in love with a man as powerful as Yuri? I guess that's my thing. Big, strong men with a soft side, except Yuri never had that softness.

I SAT BACK and wondered who my father was. So far, all I had was the name Lucky. No doubt it was a nickname. A kid growing up with that name would have been beaten to a pulp each day because of it.

I swiped at the cut on my forehead and smeared what little blood oozed from it away, then dug back in to my mom's journal. The entries were daily accounts of what was happening, from my A on a spelling test to me losing another tooth. I remembered putting that tooth under my pillow and waking up to find a dollar bill and a candy bar. I always thought it odd that the tooth fairy would give me money and something that would rot my teeth, but Mom said it was a guarantee she'd stay in business. That was the last time I got anything from the tooth fairy.

MARCH 16TH

. . .

My roses are budding. I spent the whole day pruning the branches. It aggravates Yuri that I put my hands in the soil and won't touch him. I'd lost any desire to be a real wife after he forced himself on me two weeks after Mikhail was born. Since that day, I lived in the guest suite and locked my door. Not that a lock stopped him from entering. He took what he wanted with regularity. Hard to believe I endured him for so long. If it weren't for Lucky, I would have never survived. That day in the spa changed my life forever. He'd sneak me out the back door and make love to me all day long and then sneak me back inside. Eventually, we had our own room, and we stayed there because it was safer. Yuri spent thousands on spa treatments, not even realizing he was footing the bill for my indiscretions, but I craved love, and Lucky gave it to me.

March 31st

He knows something. He's upped my security detail, which means he realizes that my time away is about something other than the appointments I claim to have. I wish he was the type of man I could be honest with. I'd love to be able to tell him that Katya isn't his child. That she's the daughter of a man I'd fallen in love with years ago. If Yuri found out I'd been cheating on him, he would have killed both Katya and me. It was safer if Lucky didn't know he was Katya's father, so I never told him. I've kept that secret for almost eight years, but life with Yuri is worse than living in a prison. I don't want this for myself or for Katya. She deserves to be happy. If I can save just a little more, I'll take her and we'll be gone.

I BRUSHED THE TEARS AWAY. *I was happy when you were alive.* My mother spoiled me. Until her death, so did my father. It all makes sense. He found out the years he'd spent doting on me were wasted on another man's offspring. I wondered if he knew who Lucky was?

APRIL 21ST

HELL, I live in hell, but at least I have a peek at heaven from my balcony. My roses are budding. I can't wait for them to bloom. It's all I have to look forward to.

The money I'd hidden is gone, which means I have no hope for escape. I don't know if it's the housekeeper or Yuri who took it. It's not like I can ask, so I smile and pretend everything is okay.

May 12th

Yuri came into my room last night and took from me what I refused to give him. I told him I'd call the police, and he told me he owned the police. What was I thinking when I said yes to him all those years ago? The reality was that back then, I knew the word no wouldn't be an acceptable answer.

Poor Katya has been knocking on my door all day, but I can't let her see me like this. I want to protect her for as long as I can. She's only a little girl.

May 28th

Katya and I had tea on the balcony. We made paper tiaras and held our pinkies high as we sipped Earl Grey and ate Irish soda bread drizzled with honey. It tickles me that she loves it so much.

She's the sweetest little girl in the world, but that's because her father's blood runs through her veins. She's so much like him in so many ways. Wicked sense of humor. Robust laugh. Eyes as blue as a summer sky. Had I made a mistake by staying with Yuri for Mikhail? As long as Yuri thinks Katya is his, she's safe. I'm safe.

June 12th

Sixteen days until my baby turns eight. She wants a pretty princess party. I've ordered Tiaras and a Cinderella dress for her birthday. Invites will go out the week before to all her classmates. Today, when I asked her if she could have anyone be her prince who would she choose, and she named the middle Wilde boy. I told her to keep that to herself because Daddy wouldn't be happy to know she'd chosen an Italian. The truth was, he hated Vince Wilde because he had what Yuri wanted. But I didn't want Katya's life to be filled with messages about hate and told her to choose wisely when she chose a prince. I wish I'd been more discerning.

June 21st

. . .

Yuri is like a caged animal today. He's burst into my room three times, demanding to know the name of the man I've been sleeping with. How he knows, I can't guess, but I'll never tell him. I've got our bags packed, and once everyone goes to sleep, Katya and I will disappear.

I READ through all six months again and memorized the details I knew for certain.

My father has blue eyes.

He is powerful but kind.

His nickname is Lucky.

He is enough for my mom to risk everything.

She died keeping his identity a secret.

I BURIED my face in my pillow and cried for over an hour. What thoughts were in my mother's head when Yuri pushed her over the balcony? I knew without a doubt she was thinking of my real father and me.

"Katya, open the damn door."

Yuri's voice snapped me out of my thoughts. He twisted the knob and pounded on the door.

"Leave me alone!" I screamed.

"Stay away from the Wildes. Do your job and

marry Sergei, and you won't meet the same fate as your mother."

Certainly, he couldn't keep me alive now that I knew the truth. I was next on his list, along with Matt. Yuri had been clear about killing him. I had to warn him.

I tucked the journal between my mattresses, slipped on a pair of sneakers, grabbed my purse, and left via my balcony. Lucky for me, I had a trellis where my mother's favorite roses climbed toward the sky as if trying to reach her.

I made my way down the thorny branches. Scraped and bleeding, I slipped into the end stall and started my car.

I didn't waste any time leaving the compound. In my rearview mirror, my prison faded until it completely disappeared. I had one objective, and that was to reach Matt. I only hoped he was sincere when he told me I belonged to him, because in ten minutes I'd land on his doorstep and he'd have to decide whether to let me and my problems inside.

CHAPTER FOURTEEN

I'd locked up the office and was walking to the apartment when Sam's cell broke the silence. He held out his hand to stop me.

"Hold," he turned to me. "Katya Petrenko is here, and she says she needs to see you." His scowl said it all. Even the hired help thought she was trouble. "She's downstairs and may be in need of first aid."

At the mention of first aid, I rushed past Sam to the elevator.

"Sir, it could be a trap. Let me go and evaluate the situation." He stood in front of the open elevator, blocking my passage.

"It's not a trap, and if she's hurt, I want to be

there for her." I shoved the big man aside and walked into the elevator. "Is she in security?"

He nodded and climbed in the elevator beside me. "You're being careless."

I turned to Sam. "I don't pay you for your opinion."

He shook his head. "No, you pay me to protect you, and I can't do that if you act impulsively."

He was right. I was acting without thought, but dammit, Katya wouldn't come here unless it was important. I stepped out of the elevator. "Bring her here straightaway. I'll take care of her."

I rushed back to the apartment and got the first aid kit from the bathroom. It was like a mini emergency room that had everything from an IV bag to antibiotics. I paced the living room for the ten minutes it took Sam to return.

When he did, my heart fell into my shoes. I rushed to Katya, who looked broken and beaten. "Oh, honey, what the hell happened to you?"

Her breaths shook her body. A whimper released when she ran to me and buried her head into my chest. "He killed my mother."

That statement pulled the floor from beneath her. She collapsed at my feet. I swooped her up and carried her to the bedroom, where I placed her on the bed and sat next to her. My poor girl was a mess. Her arms were full of scratches, like she'd crawled through brambles to escape. A cut about two inches long ran across her forehead, close to her hairline. Fury filled me. Someone was going to pay for every drop of her blood they spilled.

"Who killed your mother?"

"Yuri," the warble in her voice gutted me. In a matter of weeks, her father had taken a strong woman capable of anything and turned her into someone I didn't recognize.

"Your father killed your mother? How do you know?"

She rolled to her side so her head was in my lap. I pushed the hair from her face and wiped the tears from her cheeks.

"He's not my father."

"Yuri isn't your father?"

She shook her head and sobbed again.

I waited for the onslaught of fresh tears to stop. "No." Her hand went to the cut on her forehead. "He…he…" She swallowed hard, like the words were stuck in her throat. "He was mad at me, and he wanted to hurt me. I wore green instead of black, and he told me I was a whore just like my mother." She took in a shaky breath. "He had kept her final diary. He threw it at me and told me to read about my mother."

It was a lot to take in, and I was removed from the situation. I couldn't imagine what it would be like for Katya to realize that she's not Yuri's. "Did he tell you he killed your mother?"

"Yes, he said she wouldn't tell him who my father was, and so he pushed her over the balcony and left her there until she was found the next day."

I pulled her into my arms and hugged her. "I'm so sorry, sweetheart." She sobbed uncontrollably for the next fifteen minutes. I didn't think a person had that many tears. When she settled down, I moved her off my lap and she told me the rest of her story. When she was finished, I told her to wait there.

She grabbed at me. "Don't leave me," she begged.

"Never. I'm just getting the first aid kit so I can take care of you."

She eased her grip, and I ran so she didn't feel like I'd abandoned her.

She winced when I cleaned the cuts and scrapes, and she sighed when I applied a soothing antibiotic ointment.

"It's going to be okay," I whispered after I had her patched up and in my arms.

She shook her head. "It's never going to be okay. I don't even know who I am."

"You're Katya, and you're mine. That's all you need to know for now."

She burrowed into me and fell asleep.

When I was certain she wouldn't wake, I climbed out of the bed and went to my office to call Alex. It was late, but he needed to know that Katya was here.

The phone rang once. "You okay?"

I chuckled. Of course, he would think I'd get myself in trouble. "Yes. I'm okay, but I have a problem."

"Is she blonde, about five-foot-five and Russian?"

I kicked back in my chair and watched the monitors in front of me. Everything seemed to be running smoothly, but if I hid Katya, there was no doubt that would change.

"Yes, it's Katya. She showed up here hysterical and injured. She also said those bullets at the funeral were meant for me. She said the hit was on me but the hitman screwed it up."

"Shit." Alex let out a stream of expletives before he calmed down. "You need to stay in the casino. We can protect you there."

"I'm not going to be a prisoner in my home."

"He's lashing out at you because you're coming between him and something he wants or needs. He needs Katya to marry Sergei, and she won't do that if she's in love with you."

I'd never considered her love for me. I just assumed her feelings matched my own. I wasn't sure what I felt for her was love, but it was all-consuming.

"She's not marrying Sergei. I won't allow that to happen."

"Dammit, Matt, do you hear what you're saying? You're willing to put all of us at risk for a woman whose father is trying to kill you."

"You'd do the same for Faye." If I wanted my brother's support, I needed to hit him in the heart.

"You're right, but he's her father."

"That's something else. Yuri isn't her father." I gave my brother the shortened version of everything she told me. "I'm not giving her back to that piece of shit. You may be willing to toss her aside, but I won't. She belongs to me."

I stood and walked around the office. The shelves had been emptied of everything. Gone were the pictures of my father with the Pope and the President. There were no more antique guns or other collectibles. They were bare and waiting for me to decorate them. I ran my hand over the mahogany finish. If I closed my eyes, I could see a picture of Katya on the center shelf. Down the road, I could imagine pictures of our children flanking hers.

I knew I had him when he let out a sigh. "Do you love her?"

"Yes," I said without reservation. "I think I always have."

"Fine. Call a meeting with Sergei. It's time we took the bull by the horns. We can't win if we can't negotiate with him. No doubt he's here to stay. Keep an eye out for Yuri. I'll call Agent Holt and have him come and talk to Katya. If she can produce evidence, we can put Yuri away for good."

"She said something about a journal, but she didn't have it with her. It could be in her purse or car."

"Does she know who her father is?" I could hear Faye in the background asking questions.

"No, she only knows he goes by the name Lucky."

There was a moment of silence. "I only know

of one man who goes by Lucky. There is no way she's his daughter."

I pressed my memory but came up blank. "Who?"

"That would be Liam O'Leary."

"Holy shit. What if she is his? That's a whole other can of worms to open."

"Don't open it yet. Let's get Katya in a good place and attack this situation one thing at a time. If she is Liam's and he never knew, there will be a body count like no one's seen before. Given the fact that Sergei has a real problem with the Irish, we don't want to let that piece of information slip."

I considered his request. "I don't want to lie to Katya. Hasn't she had enough lies in her life? That asshole made her believe her mother killed herself. All this time, Katya thought she was worthless because not even her mother loved her enough to stay."

"You're not lying to her. We need to do the legwork before we start a different war."

As usual, he was right. There was no use starting something if we didn't have solid proof. "Okay, I agree. I don't want to introduce another problem into her life if it's not going to turn into something positive. We'll have to figure out a way to approach Liam."

"Leave that to me. Liam is reasonable, and his family is important to him."

"You think he'd treat Kirsten the same way Yuri treats Katya?" What I really wanted to know was, if he were her father, would he try to control her future? I didn't want her influenced by a father who didn't have her best interests at heart.

"So far, Kirsten hasn't been promised to anyone. I don't know what his thoughts on daughters and marriage are, but we're getting ahead of ourselves here. We'll need to prove she's his daughter first."

We hung up, and I sent Sam to deliver a message to Sergei. If he got it, he'd be here tomorrow night for a meeting.

I returned to Katya, who was still asleep in my bed. She was so tiny buried in the covers. I undressed and slid in next to her.

Naturally, she sought me out and curled into my body. I wrapped my arms around her and hugged her tight.

"You're mine," I told her. "I love you, and I will keep you safe."

"I'm yours," she whispered.

CHAPTER FIFTEEN

I rolled over and hit a solid mass of muscle. Naked muscle.

"Good morning, Katya." Matt's voice was slow and sexy.

When I looked up, he was propped on his elbow, staring down at me. I took him in, from the top of his head to the perfect V of his muscles that disappeared under the sheet at his hips.

"Good morning," I croaked out. Every muscle ached, from my throat to my eyeballs. Who knew I could cry so much? "Thank you for taking me in."

His lips stretched thin. "What did you expect me to do, toss you on your ass?"

I pulled the cover over my head. I felt a mess. I

knew I looked a mess. This was not the way I wanted Matt to see me.

"As a matter of fact, I did since you tossed me on my ass once this week already. Besides, I'm a mess."

He pulled the sheet from my face. "You're a beautiful mess." He pressed his lips to mine in a sweet closed mouth kiss. I tried to turn my face from him. "I mean…ackkk! Morning breath." But he cupped my cheek to keep me in place.

"I need to borrow a toothbrush if you're going to kiss me."

"I'm going to kiss you whether you brushed your teeth or not. All I want is your lips on mine." He covered my mouth with his, and all thoughts of brushing my teeth disappeared. The kiss was slow and languid, and when he pulled away, I felt the loss profoundly. "That's more like it. How are you feeling today?"

I looked down at the scratches on my arms. "Like I climbed down the trellis outside my bedroom and fell into my mom's rose bushes." The mention of my mother made my stomach twist and ache. Tears filled my eyes.

He pulled me into his arms and hugged me tightly. "I've got you."

"Don't let me go." I burrowed into his body, seeking his warmth and strength.

"Not a chance." His hands glided over my body. It wasn't sexual in any way, but comforting. "I've got to take a shower so I'm ready for my meeting this morning. Stella is in the kitchen making breakfast. She's going to fuss over you all day."

"Will you be back?"

"Yes, of course." He tilted his head. "Unless Sergei has me killed."

I sat up. "You can't meet with him." My whole body started to shake. "He's not a good man. He will kill you."

"He can try." Matt sat up and swung his legs off the mattress. That's when I saw the purple bruise on his back.

"Oh my God, your back. The bullet bruised you so badly." My fingers traced over the fist-sized purple mark. "Does it hurt?" I moved off the bed and sat beside him.

"I've felt worse." His hand rubbed along the scar where he'd been shanked in prison. He turned to me. "I have to meet with Sergei. He's not going to let you go without a fight, and I'm plain just not letting you go."

He meant it when he said I was his. "I'm not holding you to words said in distress."

He rose from the bed. The globes of his ass were solid and flexed with each step. "I'm holding you to your words whether said in distress or passion."

"I never promised anything." I stood and followed him to the bathroom.

"You said you're mine, and you are." He turned on the shower. Jets pulsed from every angle. "Are you taking that back?"

Was it possible to be his? There was nothing I wanted more. "No, but…"

He pulled off my T-shirt and tugged down my flannel pants. "But nothing. Let's get you cleaned up and fed. I'll have the gift store send up everything you'll need."

He placed his hand on my back and led me into the hot shower. The water stung the scratches on my arms, but the pulsing of the jets kneaded my sore muscles.

"You don't have to get me clothes."

He pressed me against the cold tile with his body. "I take care of what's mine."

"And I'm yours," I said to see if the words rang true and they did. I felt the certainty deep in my marrow.

He squirted body wash that smelled like lavender into his palms and rubbed it over my skin. "Tell me what you know about Sergei. I hate going into a meeting blind. I have to find something he wants bad enough to let you go for it."

How was I supposed to think with his hands gliding over me? Every nerve ending was on fire, every brain cell dead. "I can't think with your hands on me."

He laughed. "Get used to it because I can't keep my hands off you."

I figured two could play at his game, and the longer I kept him in the shower, the higher the likelihood I could get him to miss his meeting. I soaped up my hands and ran them down his body until his heavy length sat in my palms.

"As good as that feels, this isn't happening right now, sweetheart, but I'll take a rain check." He moved my hands from his shaft. "Now talk to me about Sergei."

Nothing killed desire like a conversation about Sergei Volkov. "I don't know much about him. While he seems to have a conscience one minute, he appears to have none the next. He was sent here with a purpose, but I get the feeling he has his own agenda."

Matt lathered my hair and then his. "Do you

think it's about money or power?"

"You know their type, you're woven from the same thread." While I hated to put him in the same mix as the Bratva soldiers, he was a mobster born and raised. For that matter, so was I. It might not run through my veins, but it was pounded into my head over the last twenty-four years.

"I'd like to believe I'm better."

I wrapped my arms around his waist and set my soapy head against his chest. "I know you're better, but with mafia men, money and power are one and the same."

He stepped us under the stream of water. The bubbles rinsed from our heads and pooled at our feet.

"You think he's here to kill Yuri?"

I was so happy he didn't refer to him as my father. "Yes, think about it. For years, things haven't been great. He's pulling in tons of money, but he's also lost a lot too. It all started because of me."

Matt turned off the water and stepped out of the shower. He took two soft plush towels from the cupboard and wrapped me in one while he stood gloriously naked and dripping water in front of me. If we weren't in a serious conversation, I would have dropped to my knees and licked the droplets from his body.

"Don't blame yourself."

I tucked my towel in the front so it stayed and took his towel and dried him while we spoke. "If I hadn't stolen that money, none of this would have happened. You wouldn't have been called over to find the error. There would have been no jail time. No stabbing. Maybe your father would still be alive."

He grabbed my hands, making me drop the towel and pulled me in. Standing in front of him, I looked up to his beautiful brown eyes.

"And we wouldn't be standing here together naked." He dropped one hand and plucked the towel from my body. "Now we're both naked. As for my father, you stealing from Yuri would have never kept mine alive. Yuri wanted it all."

A chill raced through me. "I think Sergei wants what Yuri has."

He turned me around and tapped my ass as he walked past me. The man had no shame, but then again, what was there to be ashamed of? The hands of the gods made him.

"He can go after Yuri for that. Would you be unhappy if Yuri met the same fate as my father?" Matt opened his drawer and handed me a T-shirt and a pair of his boxers. "Wear this for now."

I slipped on the clothes. They hung from my body but comforted me to know I wore something of his. It was like marking my territory.

"I want to kill him myself." The man deserved to be tossed out from the same balcony as my mother. He should know what it feels like to plummet to his death.

"I won't allow the future mother of my children to have his death on her hands."

He was talking about children with me. Was that even a possibility? "You don't even know if we are compatible."

He slid into a pair of black slacks and picked out a crisp white shirt. "We are. There are few things I've known for certain, and yet, you're one of them. I'm so certain that I'd take you to the drive-through-chapel and marry you today."

"You can't mean that."

He rummaged through his ties and came out with a dark red. "This is for you. I know how you love red." He lifted his collar and proceeded to put his tie on. I loved a man in a suit. There wasn't anything that looked so powerful and manly except for Matt naked.

"My brother did it. I don't see why we can't."

I reached up to straighten the crooked knot. "You suck at tying ties."

"Mrs. Price usually does it for me."

"As for the drive-through-chapel, I don't want to rush things." I stepped back and looked at Matt standing in his suit while I stood wearing his underwear. "I'd really like to find my father if I can."

A little smile lifted his lips. "You will find your father. I'm sure of it."

I got the impression that he knew something. "What do you know that I don't?"

"I know nothing but what you told me." He threaded his fingers through mine and walked me down the hallway to the kitchen, where the air smelled like bacon and maple syrup.

In seconds, I was in the arms of Stella. "You poor thing. Matt tells me you need some mothering."

I looked at him, and he winked. He grabbed a piece of bacon and kissed me on the cheek. "I'll be back around dinner. Don't leave the apartment. I'll send someone up with clothes. They'll call you for your sizes." He was already dialing someone on his phone as he walked away.

Stella led me to the table in the kitchen and pointed to the spot that was set for one. "You can eat in the dining room if you prefer, but Matt hates eating alone. I thought maybe we can get to know each other over coffee and breakfast." She poured me a cup of black coffee and dosed it with cream. "Matt says you like more cream than coffee."

I was touched by how much he knew about me. We went to the same school, we socialized in the same circles, but I never knew he paid that much attention. Maybe he was right and we were meant for each other.

"Thank you."

She filled my plate with pancakes and bacon. "Mangia," she said with gusto. "You must eat if you're ever going to fatten up."

"Fatten up?"

Stella stood beside me and shook her head. "You're so thin, you could hula hoop with a Cheerio."

I took a bite of the bacon and hummed at the crunchy salty goodness. "I'm not that thin."

She pinched my cheek and smiled. "I'll plump you up so you're healthy enough to have fat little babies." She picked up the syrup and drowned my pancakes in it.

"Why is my uterus so popular?" This was the second time today babies were mentioned.

"It's those eyes. They'll look so good on our babies."

Her enthusiasm was contagious. I'd never been around women who were mothering and nurturing. All I had to go by was the love of a mother who died too young.

When I tried to eat a few bites and push the plate away, Stella stomped her foot and told me I owed her five more bites. I was certain she'd spoon-feed me if I didn't comply.

Stuffed to the hilt, I waddled into the living room. The wall of windows looked over the city. From this high up, the cars looked so small. The phone rang, and Stella asked my size. A half-hour later, we were rummaging through a rack of clothes brought up by a cute redhead who worked in the boutique downstairs.

"This one," Stella said as she held out the red sundress. "Matt says you love red."

Again, the man knew way too much about me. I tried it on and found it a perfect fit.

Stella pulled most of the clothes off the rack and placed them in the closet. She'd organized the space so one side was Matt's and the other mine. By lunchtime, it looked like I'd lived there forever.

"Come and eat," she called from the kitchen.

"I don't eat lunch."

"You do now." She pulled out my chair, and I sat down in front of a plate of lasagna and a glass of red wine.

"This is good for you and our babies."

"I'm not pregnant."

"Not yet, but you will be." She sat across from me and joined me for lunch. "What else do you need? I've sent for makeup and the essentials women must have because we are women."

I swallowed the best lasagna I've ever tasted. "What do you consider essentials?"

She smiled. "Perfume, accessories, makeup, sexy lingerie." She lifted the skirt of my dress to show Matt's boxers. "These will never do. It's like trying to lure a honeybee with tar."

Laughter bubbled inside me. It had been too long since I'd spent time with a woman. Sure I had Darya and her mother at the house, but they weren't allowed to talk to me in the way Stella did. My father separated what he called the grain from the chaff, as if somehow we were valuable and the help was inferior.

"Matt doesn't seem to mind."

"No, but that boy's been in prison for too long."

Guilt stabbed at my insides. If I was going to

be a part of Matt's life, then the people he cared about needed to know the truth.

"You should know that I sent him to prison."

She wiped her face with her napkin. "I know. You put him there because even then you loved him." She said it with such conviction.

"I'm not sure it was love, but I cared about him."

She stood up and cleared our plates. "It was love. Even then, your heart knew what your mind could not accept."

"We came from rival families."

"You came from mafia families, and that is not your fault."

She was right. I was not my father. Or at least the father I knew and hated. I was Katya Petre… no, I was simply Katya, and that would have to be enough for now.

CHAPTER SIXTEEN

There was no way I'd let Sergei get close to Katya, so I had Mrs. Price set up a conference room in the hotel. I arrived fifteen minutes early to find my brother and his security detail already in place.

"I've got extra men on the doors. Tony will stand guard outside. Since there are two of us, Sergei can bring in a man if he wants to even the numbers."

It didn't matter that Alex was the one who desperately wanted out of the business; he still acted like the Godfather when it came to our safety.

"What do you know about him?" I knew Alex

would have someone dig up everything they could.

"He's thirty-five. Never been married. Hates the Irish. Moved up in rank quickly because of his vicious nature. If he can't talk you out of what he wants, he'll kill you to get it. Word on the street is, he wants the territory. Did Katya tell you anything?"

I thought about the hours I held her last night. The tears she spilled over her lost family. How Yuri had played with her life as if it held no more importance than a poker chip.

"She said the same. That he might look like he had a conscience but to not let that influence me. He was after everything and would do what it took to get it."

"So basically he would have married her. Killed Yuri, got her pregnant and then she would have disappeared."

Hearing it all lined out as if it was the directions to a recipe for success made the bile rise in my throat.

"He will never get his hands on her. Never stick his dick inside her. She's mine."

"Got it." He walked to the table and took a seat. "I guess Dad's message of if it floats, flies or fucks, then rent it didn't resonate with either of us."

"Why rent when it can own you?" I laughed because even though my sentence was said in jest, it was true. One time being inside of Katya had me hooked. One night sleeping with her in my arms had me reeled in for life. That woman owned me. I'd be smart not to let her catch on.

The door swung open, and two men walked inside. I recognized them both from Capone's and the funeral. I turned to my brother. "Let me introduce you to Sergei."

"I assume since there are two of you, it's okay for me to have Timur present." He looked at the man who was as big as a mountain.

"Of course. This is a friendly meeting." I walked over to the table by the wall. "Shall we table our weapons?"

The men looked at each other and followed me. I took my Glock from my waistband and set it on the table. Alex did the same. We were leaving ourselves vulnerable as a show of good faith. If things turned south, the reality was, Sergei might get a shot off but Tony and Sam and the others would finish them off. No one would leave here alive if a shot was fired.

Timur took a gun from his belt, one from his

ankle, brass knuckles from his pocket and a knife from his sock. Alex and I looked on in surprise. Sergei pulled out a few surprises as well. He had two guns. One tucked into his belt and another strapped to a holster inside his shirt.

"Did you come prepared for a war?" I asked.

Sergei laughed, "No, if I thought it was war, I would have armed myself better."

I led the men to the table in the center of the room.

"I invited you here so we could negotiate."

"Did you sleep with my future wife last night?" His voice was tinged with humor.

"Yes, I did, but she will never be your wife. You don't want her, but I do."

Sergei lifted his shoulders. "I do want her, but not in the way you do. We could come to an arrangement. She will marry me and sleep with you."

Heat of agitation boiled in my veins. "You want her to bear you a child. I will not have you raise my son. Katya deserves more than to be whored out by Yuri or you."

"You love my fiancée?" He smiled that damn arrogant smile that said I'd given him the power.

"Love has nothing to do with it. Katya is not

property to be traded. She's a human being and a good woman."

Timur and Sergei looked at each other, and they both laughed. "It is sad she was born a girl. Her choices don't matter. You should know that. In our world, she's a commodity. She's Yuri's daughter and born to be wed and bred."

It took all my self-control not to fist up and throw a punch. "What if I said she's not Yuri's daughter?"

Sergei's eyes grew wide. "Of course she is. Why would he raise someone else's bastard?"

"Revenge." Alex said. "As it turns out, Katya is not Yuri's daughter. He told her as much yesterday after the funeral. He gave her her mother's journal, which proved Katya belonged to another man. Then he told her how he callously killed her mother by throwing her off the balcony. Katya was almost eight. It's not like he could make her disappear when people would have asked questions. He couldn't kill her, because that would have been suspicious, so he raised her as his and planned to use her to get our holdings."

Alex told him of the plot to take out the Wildes one at a time.

I stepped in and added a spin on the truth. I reached into my pocket and grabbed the printout of Yuri's financials. In yellow highlighter, I had circled what I knew to be a hit on me. If I were lucky, Sergei wouldn't be privy to that information.

"This here is the payment for a hit on you."

Timur turned red in the face. Sergei fisted his hands and pounded on the table. "How do you know?"

"Are you asking how I got this information, or how do I know it's a hit?"

He frowned. "I'm asking both."

I smiled. "I'm a hacker. It's what started all this shit to begin with." Katya was right in one sense. The day I found her money trail was the day it all began for us, but it wasn't her fault. It was Yuri's. He started this the day he killed Katya's mother.

I filled Sergei in on the history. Of course, I left out the parts about Katya stealing Yuri's money. There was no reason to implicate her.

"Katya has these skills too?"

I laughed. "No, she can probably open a door remotely or maybe get inside your computer to rifle around. I'd say she could even bypass an alarm system, but hack into a bank? No." She didn't have the same set of skills I had. Hell, I'd hacked into the IRS once and erased all the tax information for my favorite teacher while also requesting an audit on the asshole who tried to give me a C in chemistry.

Sergei and Timur exchanged words in Russian. "None of this matters."

Those were his words, but the way Timur's eyes turned black meant it mattered plenty.

"It matters because if he kills you, then everything you're after is gone. You are after everything, right?"

I gave him an I've-got-your-number look. "I will have everything."

I cleared my throat. "Everything but Katya. She's off the table. Hell, she may not even be in the will." I hadn't considered that, but I imagine there was no way Yuri would leave anything to a daughter who didn't share his gene pool. "He's not going to leave her anything, so she's worthless to you." I took the printouts that sat in front of Sergei, folded them and stuck them in my pocket.

He gave me a serial killer smile. "That's where you're wrong. She's worth everything to you, so that gives her value. What will you give up for her?"

Here it was. This is where the rubber met the road. "What do you want?" I figured if I could make him walk away for cash, I'd be lucky.

"That's simple. I want everything."

Alex pushed back and stood. Timur postured himself by pressing his palms to the table. He was in ready to go into fight mode.

"He wants what Yuri wanted. He wants the casino," Alex said.

"No deal," I replied. "It's not for sale or trade."

Sergei laughed. "But Katya is, or so it would seem."

I hated that she'd become a commodity. That somehow she could be bartered and traded like a possession.

"What do you want?"

"If I can't have the casino, then I expect you to hand over my fiancée."

"You don't love her, you don't care about her. Just let her go. I'll help you get what you want. I can use my skills to get you places you could only imagine."

"No!" my brother yelled. "We are out of the business."

Sergei looked between us. "Looks like that's changed. You owe me, and you owe my family. You've stolen my fiancée, and you killed my cousin. Those are enormous debts that must be paid." He rose and walked to the table to get his weapons. Timur followed suit. "I'll be in touch."

They walked out of the room.

"What the hell were you thinking?" Alex yelled. "You played right into his hand, and now he has you by the gonads."

"Maybe. Maybe not. Everyone has something to hide, Sergei does too. I have to find the skeleton in his closet. He's got to have a weak spot as well."

"You better find it fast because we have less than three weeks before the shit goes down. Sergei intends to claim everything. You can see it in his eyes. He'll stop at nothing until he has it all."

Alex was right. Sergei had soulless eyes. We walked back to the table and grabbed our weapons. Alex headed home to Faye while I took the elevator up to my apartment.

"Stay there," Stella said as I walked inside. She rushed to the dining room, the lights dimmed, and the flicker of candlelight danced on the walls.

The air was filled with the scent of garlic and cheese and something sweet like flowers.

"Okay, you can come in," Stella waved me into the formal dining room that was set for two. She leaned over and kissed me on the cheek. "She made dinner with my help. Make sure you praise her. I get the feeling she doesn't hear good things often." She walked out of the dining room, and I heard the front door click shut.

In front of me was a bottle of cabernet airing. I filled the two wine glasses and waited. Her soft footsteps sounded behind me.

"I'm so glad you're safe. I was worried about you." She moved to my side and placed a platter of spaghetti and meatballs on the table, but that's not what I noticed most. She was dressed in red. Her hair was done. Her makeup was on. Those damn lips looked kissable. This wasn't the Katya normally filled with anxious energy. She didn't look like a deer in the headlights, ready to bolt. She looked at peace.

CHAPTER SEVENTEEN

This was far too domestic for it to be my reality. I hadn't eaten a family dinner since the night my mother died. I'd never cooked a meal in my life unless toasting a bagel counted. Here I stood in front of Matt like it was normal for me to cook his meal—normal for us to sit at the massive table—normal for us to act like a family. None of this was normal, but I wanted it to be.

There had been so much talk about babies that as I looked down the table, I could see little Italian boys with their dad's dark hair and brown eyes.

"You cooked?" He lifted a brow.

I took the seat to his right. Stella told me I

should always sit to my man's right. It was a position of power, and it said something about my place in his life. It gave the saying '*his right-hand man*' some weight. I wanted to be Matt's right-hand woman.

"I helped cook." Stella showed me how to make her sauce from tomatoes and spices. She gave me her secret meatball recipe. She told me the key was to make sure the balls weren't rolled too tightly, otherwise, the sauce couldn't season them.

Matt served me first and then put a healthy mound on his plate. "I'm impressed."

"Don't be until you taste it. It could be crap." I spun my fork around until it was circled in spaghetti.

He took a bite, and his eyes opened wide. He smiled and nodded. "So good."

I beamed at his praise. Never had I nailed something the first try, but after my bite, I agreed. This was damn good pasta.

"How did the meeting go?"

"It was crap. He wants the casino in exchange for you."

I gasped. "You told him no, right? I'm not worth that much. I'm worthless, actually." My chin fell. "At least when I was Yuri's daughter, I had the power of the Petrenko name behind me. Now I don't know who I am. I could be the gardener's kid, for all I know."

"Isn't your gardener Hispanic?"

I laughed. "No, he's Japanese."

He looked at my distinctive European features. "You're definitely not his daughter."

"Probably not. About the casino…"

"While I believe you are worth far more than Old Money Casino, I did not barter my family legacy for you. I will figure out a way for us to be together."

"Okay, but it has to be a way that doesn't involve murder or an Elvis Presley wedding."

He offered me his hand in a shake. "That's a deal."

We finished our dinner and took the bottle of wine to the living room.

"I love your place. It's so big and open and airy." I'd had plenty of time to explore. I'd even sat at his desk for an hour today, hoping to get a glimpse of him in one of the monitors, but I never did.

"It's a great place. I'm not sure it's my forever place. Why my father wanted to work and live here is beyond me. I imagine he left the house so he wasn't haunted by memories of my mom."

"Did you sell the house?"

"No, we gave it to Rafe. I got the apartment and run the casino. Alex is in charge of the property development company, and Rafe will keep us out of trouble when he gets back."

Matt sat on the leather sofa and patted the cushion next to him. I happily snuggled into his side. I felt vulnerable and raw, but when he was near, I was safe.

"Where is he?"

"With all the stuff going down and Yuri putting the hit on me, we thought it was a good idea if he took a vacation. He's waiting on his bar exam results but should be back with a tan in a week or so."

"I'm sorry my family has caused you so many problems."

He set his wine glass down and pulled me into his lap. "You have nothing to do with it. You're an innocent bystander."

I laid my head on his shoulder. "I'm not always that innocent."

"I like your bad side. You're like one of those German chocolate eggs. You break it open and never know what surprise you'll find inside."

"Speaking of surprises, I still can't believe how much my life has changed since yesterday. What's worse is, Yuri hasn't come looking for me. That worries me."

"Yuri is a problem, but he'll be taken care of. Do you have your mother's journal?"

It never occurred to me to bring it with me. Not that I could have maneuvered down the trellis with it tucked under my chin anyway, but I could have tossed it to the lawn and got it when I climbed down. *Stupid. Stupid. Stupid.*

"No, it's in my room."

"Damn," the gruff word rumbled in his chest. "That was the smoking gun."

"It didn't say much of anything. All it did was spark a lot of questions."

Matt sat forward to get his wine, and I reluctantly moved off his chest.

"That's what we need. While the crime is too old to prosecute, we could get Agent Holt to use it as a way to get nosy, and hopefully, he'd find something else while he was snooping around."

While I didn't want to go back to the house, I would if I had to. "I'll go get it."

Matt tabled his wine and gripped my shoulders. "No, you won't. I don't want you anywhere near Sergei or Yuri. Neither one of them cares about you, but they will both use you."

I moved to the edge of the sofa and turned toward him. "I'm no longer worth anything to them. Did you tell Sergei that I wasn't Yuri's daughter?"

He nodded. "He still expects to marry you because I believe like he does that's what Yuri told you in the heat of anger, but he doesn't want anyone else to know. If he thinks like my father did, he'll kill anyone who does to save face."

I laughed. "He'd have a hell of a time killing Sergei. Men surround him all the time. I swear Timur is stuck to his hip. He's never more than a few feet away. Then there's you. If killing all who know is his plan, he'll try to kill you again." A tear slipped from my eye.

"He won't kill me. I'm like a cat, and I've only used a few lives so far. Don't worry."

Matt lifted me to straddle his lap. He leaned forward to lick the tear from my cheek. A delicious shudder ran down my spine. I shimmied forward so our hips touched and his length sat trapped hard and needy between us.

His hands skimmed my body from hips to back. Nimble fingers unzipped the back of my dress and let it fall off my shoulders.

"Why are we talking about Yuri when we can be making love?"

With his hands cupping my breasts, I couldn't

think of one reason to discuss Yuri. I loosened his tie, unbuttoned his shirt and let my fingertips dance across his chest. Up and down, I memorized every hill and valley of muscle that made up the man I loved. I shifted away until I could slide to the floor in front of him.

Heavy lidded, his long lashes sat on his cheeks while I unbuckled, unbuttoned and unzipped his pants. When I pulled his length free and wrapped my lips around him, his body turned to butter on the soft leather sofa.

His gruff voice began to hum with the sounds of satisfaction as I took him inside the heat of my mouth.

"Perfect. So damn perfect," he said as his fingers threaded through my hair. He never once demanded I change the depth or pace. He enjoyed what I gave him without taking anything. It was such an odd concept for me. I'd never been given the option to give freely.

His body tensed. The muscles of his thighs tightened. In a swift move, he pulled me up and lifted us both from the couch. With my legs wrapped around his waist, he carried us to the bed, and within minutes I was naked and he was inside of me. Only this time it wasn't desperate, but slow and steady and purposeful.

I knew once again that every stroke was a message to my mind, body, and soul that I belonged to him.

When we lay sated and sweaty in each other's arms, I knew no other truth. While I never wanted to be given away like a piece of property, I was happy to give myself to Matt.

When his breathing became deep and steady, I slipped from the bed. In the dark of the night, I cleaned up the kitchen and tried to figure out a way to sneak back into the house without risking my life or limb.

In the early morning hours, I crawled back into bed and curled into the body of the only man who tried to protect me.

THE DAYS PASSED IN A BLUR. The closer my wedding day got, the deeper the lines on Matt's face drew. I knew things were tense by the number of men who showed up to guard the floor we stayed on. Matt used to have only Sam, but now there were guards everywhere. They seemed to come out of the woodwork with each passing day.

When I walked into the kitchen, I found Matt

on the phone. He didn't notice my presence, so I stopped to listen.

"Hey Alex, I wanted to tell you we got robbed last night."

My hand came to my mouth to stifle a gasp. I pulled out of sight completely because I knew if Matt saw me, he'd end the call, and I wanted more information.

"It was Yuri."

My fists knotted up. If the man was in front of me, I'd kill him without a second thought to anything.

"I know it was him because he left an itemized bill at the cage where his men took the precise amount of $86,732.00. He's charged me $5000 a day for the company of Katya and took back the money I donated in his name to charity, which was $15,000 plus additional interest he thought fair."

What man sells his daughter for $5000 a day? Then I remembered I wasn't his daughter, but a piece of property he'd been bartering with all my life. This had to stop. Somehow, I'd find a way out so I could get the journal. Tonight was the night. Being in the penthouse, there wasn't a trellis for me to slip down, so I had to get creative.

I made some noise as I turned the corner into the kitchen. Matt swung around to look at me. Though his forehead was marred with the lines of worry, his downturned lips lifted into a bright smile.

"I've got to go." He ended the call and wrapped his arms around me.

"Who was that?" I breathed him into my lungs. In case things didn't go as I planned tonight, I'd need to have something to remember. I loved the way his skin tasted like sugar and smelled like citrus.

"It was Alex. We were going over the financials."

"You don't have to lie to me. I realize me being here has put you all at risk."

Matt stepped back. "You being here has been the best thing to happen to me."

"You're the best thing that has ever happened to me too. I love you, Matt. I want you to know that in case things get ugly."

He cupped my face and pressed his lips to mine. "You love me?" he asked as he pulled away.

"Yes, I think I've loved you since I was a little girl and you rode that black pony at my party. I told my mom that day you'd be my prince. She laughed at me. She knew that was going to be impossible. At that time, I didn't understand anything about our life."

"Nothing is impossible, sweetheart. You have to want it enough. You have to be willing to risk everything to get what's important to you."

I tenderly kissed him. "I am." What he didn't realize was, a few hours after we'd make love tonight, I'd sneak out of bed and go back into the lions' den to get what I needed to hopefully bury Yuri.

"Me too. I'll do anything to keep you."

That was what I was afraid of.

"How about room service and a movie?"

I ordered a ton of stuff I knew we wouldn't eat, but that was part of my plan. Lot's of stuff meant they'd roll in a table. A table that would also need to be rolled away, and if I was lucky, I'd be able to climb inside to make my escape.

CHAPTER EIGHTEEN

While Katya perused the room service menu, I rewound the security footage and watched Yuri's men boldly enter the casino, walk up to the cashier's cage and abscond with close to a hundred grand. They stared straight into the cameras and smiled.

One of them flipped me off before he took the money and walked out. They knew no one would call the police because any connection to the mob would bring the Feds in, and I didn't need them snooping around. We were running a clean operation now, but I still had years of books to doctor in case something happened and we were audited or our financial records were seized. Dad hadn't been that diligent. He was the kind of guy who would deal with the punches as they came. I preferred to be prepared, so I let Yuri's goons walk out free and clear.

Ultimately, the joke was on him. I'd have paid ten times that amount for each night with Katya. Hell, I was getting ready to turn my back on my family for her.

I closed my office door to make my next call. My gut twisted when Sergei answered the phone.

"I knew you would call. You seem like a smart man."

"You seem like an asshole."

Sergei let out a belly laugh so loud, I had to pull the phone from my ear.

"It would appear we're both accurate," he said.

"Here's the deal. I won't give you the casino, but I will give you the deal my father gave Yuri. I'll hold your high stakes gaming, launder your money, and serve your watered down alcohol to my patrons. In exchange, you'll break off the marriage to Katya and get Yuri on the same page. There won't be another offer coming, so take it or leave it."

"I'll take it, but…I want something else. I want something for Dima's death."

"I didn't kill Dima; he killed himself." I had the coroner's report on my computer and pulled it up and pressed send to Sergei. "Your cousin was a sick bastard. He got off on cutting up women. He got what he gave to others and couldn't live with it. I'm not giving you anything for his life."

I heard the ding of the incoming message through the phone. There was silence while I imagined he read the report.

"It makes no matter how he died. He wasn't supposed to die."

"Neither was my father, so that makes us even."

"I didn't kill your father," Sergei replied.

"And I didn't kill Dima." Not to say I wouldn't have. I was not like Alex; I had blood and lives on my hands, but the people I killed always deserved it. I wouldn't have blinked an eye at killing that bastard. "If we want to compare apples to apples, you're in debt to me because your boss had me shanked in prison. You owe me, asshole."

There was a grunt on the line before he spoke. "Yuri is not my boss. I will deal with him. You will answer to me."

"Now you're delusional. I'll never answer to you. You heard my deal, take it or leave it. Dima for Vince. The other stuff for Katya. You won't talk to her, or look or her, or contact her again. Final offer."

Sergei spoke Russian to someone and then growled. “Deal.”

When I hung up the phone, I knew I’d made a deal with the devil, but I did it because I was in love with an angel.

My next call went to Alex, who had met with Liam tonight. Part of me prayed he wasn’t Katya’s father, the other part hoped he was because as far as mobsters went, Liam was at least fair. My only concern was Katya going from one mafia family to the next when all she wanted was to be free of the life. Sadly, in saving her, I’d made sure we were in for the long haul.

“What do you know?” I asked when Alex answered.

The silence ate me up.

“I hope you like Guinness, because the timeline matches. Turns out Liam met Anya at the spa. She knew who he was, but she also loved him despite it all. He’d asked her to leave Yuri early on. She wouldn’t because of Mikhail. He didn’t know about Katya. They had ended their affair long before her birth.”

“So my little Russian is actually an Irish hellion with a Russian accent.”

Alex chuckled. “She’s half-Russian and half-

Irish. That's a dangerous mix. Are you sure you can handle it?"

"God help me. What about Liam, does he want proof?" I had no idea how I'd get it to him, but I would if he required it.

"Yep, he wants DNA evidence before he steps into the picture. He knows once word gets out, all hell will break loose between the Russians and the Irish. If she is his daughter and you intend on keeping her, then that will stir up stuff as well. Her marriage to you isn't one that will bring something to the organization, and because you're my brother and Faye's my wife, there will always be the distrust since Faye's father is FBI. Boy, we know how to create turmoil."

I thought about my deal with Sergei and wondered if I should come clean now, but it seemed more important to tell my brother face to face. I owed him that much, especially since he'd removed us from our life of crime. Of course, he could walk away, but I knew he wouldn't; we were like the damn musketeers, and the all for one and one for all motto would be lived.

"What's the plan? Will they meet and give blood? How does he want to do this?"

"He doesn't want to rock the boat until he knows for certain. All I need is a piece of hair, preferably from the root. I'll set up the testing, just get me what I need."

Hair was easy. Hell, that woman's DNA was everywhere, from my shower to my sheets.

A knock at the door interrupted my thoughts. I got up and opened it to find Katya dressed in my T-shirt and boxers. Behind her was a room service table full of dessert, but my eyes went straight to the can of whipped cream.

"Got to go," I told my brother. "Dessert just arrived."

I picked Katya up and tossed her over my shoulder. I swiped the whipped topping off the tray on my way to our room. She wanted dessert and a movie. I'd satisfy her sweet tooth first.

An hour later, we stood in the shower, rinsing off the stickiness that we hadn't licked clean from each other's bodies. I spied a single hair standing up and plucked it from her scalp.

"Ouch," she rubbed the spot. "Why did you do that?"

I pressed the strand to the tile for later retrieval. "It was sticking up." I pushed her against the wall until my length slid through her thighs.

She reached down and gripped my shaft. "This is sticking up. Should I pluck it from your body?"

"You can try." I lifted her into my arms and pressed myself inside her body. "But I think this is a better use for my part than having it plucked from between my legs." I slid in and out of her heat. There was no place I'd rather be than deep inside Katya. I knew I'd won the argument when she moaned and covered my mouth with a kiss. It didn't take her long before she shattered in my arms. I loved it when she gave everything over to me.

CHAPTER NINETEEN

My legs felt like noodles after our first round of dessert. Tucked up next to Matt with a plate of berry cobbler in my hands, I waited for him to choose a movie. Of all the movies we could watch, he chose *Married to the Mob.*

"Seriously?" I lunged for the remote, but he held it out of my reach.

"I want to see if they got it right."

"It's Hollywood. There's no way it's right."

He stole my next bite and pressed play. "At least we can laugh at what they got wrong."

And so we did. We laughed so hard that my stomach hurt.

Matt pushed the room service table toward

the door, but I stopped him. "I might want some of this in the morning." I lifted the lid to a tray of cookies and a slice of chocolate cake. "I'll take care of it tomorrow."

He smiled. "Good idea. You need some fattening up. Stella tells me I have to plump you up before my seed plumps you up."

"Stella would be happy if I gained half my body weight." I walked into the bathroom to brush my teeth and look into the mirror. I'd definitely put a few pounds on since I moved in with Matt, but he didn't seem to mind. With each pound I gained, he wanted me more.

I climbed into bed and curled into his side. It would have been easy to fall asleep, but I had to protect what we had, and the only way to do that was to get the journal and hope it opened the door to questions.

When Matt's deep breaths turned into a soft snore, I snuck from the bed and dressed. I knew there would be a guard at the elevator, but I also knew that he'd let room service clear the table if the call came from Matt or me.

With my keys and my phone in my pocket, I called for a pick up and pushed the cart into the hallway. After I waved at the guard by the elevator, I disappeared under the tablecloth to ball up on the shelf below. It took the guy thirty minutes to get there and another ten to get me down to the kitchen. When I heard no one near the table, I popped from my hiding space and walked out the back of the hotel. No one noticed because they were busy receiving deliveries. Trucks lined up around the block to deliver the food and alcohol needed to sustain an establishment of this size. No wonder Yuri wanted this place so badly.

A warm wonderful feeling came over me. Matt loved me. He said he'd keep me safe. I loved Matt, and the only way to keep him safe was to exterminate Yuri. While I didn't want to kill anyone, I wouldn't give Yuri a second thought if he got in my way. I'd suffered since my mother's death. The bastard believed in an eye for an eye. What about a life for a life? He took my mother's from her. Yuri had to pay.

The valet brought my car around. I knew if something happened to me, Matt would see me on the camera, so I mouthed the words I wanted him to remember, "I love you," and I drove away. I parked outside the compound. There was one place where a person could scale the wall and not be seen. I knew of this place because it was how I snuck out as a teenager. The ivy was so thick along the inner perimeter that I'd carved out a path. No doubt the gardener saw the tunnel that ran beneath the vines, but he never said a word.

Once inside, I moved through the vines and spider webs until I reached the servants' entrance. Hopefully, Darya still had the bad habit of smoking. She came out the side entrance so often that she rarely bothered to lock the door. I bounded up the steps and turned the knob. I was in.

Dressed in a pair of rubber-soled sneakers, I tiptoed up the back staircase to the corridor that led to Yuri's room. If I'd been braver, I'd have grabbed a knife from the kitchen and shoved it into his cold heart as I passed his room. Instead, I silently passed his room and prayed that Karma would be the equalizer.

The house was deadly silent as I made my way to my room. I inhaled the scent of lemon cleaner and my perfume. Nothing seemed to have changed from the day I'd left. The maid had cleaned. My computer still sat open on the desk. It was as if I'd never been gone.

I dropped to my knees and felt between my mattresses for the journal. My fingers wrapped around the stiff binding. My heart leaped for joy. With luck, I could get out and be back in bed before Matt noticed I was gone.

I glanced around the room that had been both

my safe haven and my cell. After spending the last few weeks with Matt, it was hard to believe I'd lived here at all. There was little I wanted but the journal and my computer and the scrap of ribbon that my mother gave me.

I gathered the items and put them in an old backpack from college. Hard to believe Yuri paid for classes. I'd gotten a useless degree as an event planner. Useless until I had to plan my own wedding in less than a day. I let the thought go and gave my room one last look before I stepped into the hallway. Across from me was Sergei's room.

I heard the groans and moans and wondered if he were sick or ill. While I owed him nothing, I did recognize that he could have come after me. My loyalties warred inside of me. I needed to get home to Matt, but I realized that Matt and I wouldn't have a chance if Sergei didn't take over the Russian holdings. Left to Yuri, everyone would be exterminated one by one.

I rocked between moving my things back to my room and looking in on Sergei and rushing to the exit. When a loud cry-like moan came from his room, I tucked my bag under my bed and walked silently across the landing. Thankfully, the key was still tucked inside the planter. I considered knocking but decided I'd sneak a peek inside. Maybe Yuri had injured him and he needed medical care. Surely, I could peek inside and assess the situation to make the correct call.

With the skill of a cat burglar, I slid the key inside the lock and turned the knob. The room was dark except for the moonlight that washed a swath of light across the bed. When my eyes adjusted and focused, what I saw answered all my questions.

In front of me was Sergei, naked with his lover's legs on his shoulders. His hips plunged forward at a brisk pace. The moans I heard were not from pain or poisoning, but from passion. Timur's hands cupped Sergei's face. The two men, lost in their passion, didn't notice me. Sergei stilled and let out a sound that could only be described as pure bliss.

I slipped out the door and back to my room. I'd stepped into something that would most definitely get me killed. I picked up my backpack and snuck down the hallway. Twenty feet more, and I'd be at the back staircase and one flight away from freedom. What I didn't expect was to turn the corner and stare into the barrel of a gun. Yuri blocked my escape.

"Nice to have you back," Yuri said in Russian.

I stumbled until I hit the wall behind me.

Yuri grabbed me by the arm and dragged me toward the grand staircase both Sergei's and my room flanked.

"Sergei can take care of you once and for all."

When we got there, Yuri pressed me against the iron railing until I was bent over backward. If not for the one foot I had wedged between the bars, I would have fallen to my death. There would have been no need to call Sergei.

"Let me go. I have information for you, but you can't call Sergei," I whispered. "It's about him, and he will kill both of us if he finds out I knew and told you." Turning the tables was the only choice I had. If I got Yuri to listen to me, he'd go after Sergei. By the way Sergei made love to Timur, I knew he'd do anything to protect his secret. Maybe they'd kill each other and I'd be free of them both.

He looked at me and then towards Sergei's door as if he was debating the lesser of two evils. Thankfully, it appeared I'd won when he yanked me forward and dragged me down the stairs like a rag doll. Even though the marble dug into my shins as I half-walked and half-fell down the grand staircase, I didn't make a sound.

When we got to the office, he pushed me forward and I landed on my knees with my backpack in front.

"What did you steal from me?" He ripped the backpack from my hands and tossed the contents on his desk. There wasn't much. It was my computer, the journal and a frayed red ribbon.

"Nothing, I came back for the only things that belonged to me." While I didn't want to put such importance on the journal and the ribbon, they were the only items I had of my mother's, and I'd feel their loss almost as profoundly as her death. I stood tall with my back straight. Yuri Petrenko scared the shit out of me, but he fed on weakness, and I'd learned to hide mine.

I lifted the backpack flap and shoved my two prized possessions inside, then opened my computer as if I had something to show him. Of course, I didn't. What I saw, I couldn't un-see, but I also didn't have proof.

"I'm not giving you any information until you call off the hit on Matt."

Yuri loomed over me like a black cloud. "You're not in a position to negotiate. One pull of the trigger, and you're gone." He rested his gun on my shoulder, making sure the barrel pointed at an angle to send a bullet through my skull. As much as my insides shook, I refused to let him see my fear.

"You don't want to do that. You wouldn't last a day if you killed me. The Wildes would have you buried a foot under in the desert."

"Only a foot?"

I smiled. "Yes, they'd hate to put you so deep that the animals would have to work hard to eat you." I typed in what I needed to get into Yuri's financial records. "You really need to get some help. A high school computer geek could infiltrate your system." I shook my head.

When I pulled up the withdrawal for waste disposal, I turned to the man who should have been protecting me all my life. "Call it off."

Yuri dropped his hand to his side, which meant I'd won this round. If I could get out of here with my head still attached, I'd be lucky.

Yuri picked up the phone and pushed a single number. Who had a hitman on speed dial? Probably every mafia boss out there, but I'd never considered the possibility. I'd known my "father" wielded a lot of power, but never had I considered a killer attached to his favorites list.

He told the person on the other end to cancel the job, then he hung up. "It's done, now tell me what you know."

"Sergei never wanted to marry me." I lifted my brows and waited.

"No surprise, look at you. You dress like a pauper, and you look like a whore."

I rubbed my sweaty palms on the shredded jeans that probably cost Matt hundreds of dollars. "It kills you that I look like my mother, doesn't it?" I was playing with fire when it came to the topic of my mom, but I owed her justice.

"You're lucky I didn't kill you because you looked like your mother. Don't think that it hadn't crossed my mind."

"I'm sure you plotted my demise every day of your life. It must have been pure joy when the Bratva told you I'd belong to Sergei."

"Happy to be rid of you, for sure."

"Unhappy to find out you'd get us both. That was the deal, right? You screwed it all up. You weren't supposed to go after the Wildes, and when you did, it was considered going rogue. Sergei is here to decide if you should live or die."

I knew I'd hit the nail on the head when his skin went a shade of white I'd never seen on him.

"What do you know about our business?"

I smiled. "I know you're a screw-up." I braced myself for the slap I'd get. "It's probably why my mother cheated on you. I can spot a loser a mile away. It's my superpower. I must have inherited that trait from her." The slap didn't sting as much as I thought because I knew my words stabbed him in the heart. "Do you know who my father is?"

Wouldn't it be nice if he blurted out a name? It could have been the devil himself, and I would have been happy as long as Yuri's blood didn't flow through my veins.

"Some fucker named Lucky. I'd say he was lucky because I made sure he wasn't saddled with your mother either. Now, what do you have on Sergei?"

My heart jolted and raced. Did I dare tell him that Sergei was gay? To out him would take away my power. I had to come up with something.

"You're dead. He's already decided." It wasn't a lie. There was no doubt in my mind that Sergei would kill us both. "The plan was to marry me and kill you. He assumed I was the sole heir." I laughed at the absurdity of my situation. "You thought the Wildes had Mikhail killed? We both know he didn't hang himself, but we also know that it cost a lot of money for people to say so. Sergei has the backing of the Bratva." I watched Yuri's face twist into a pained expression. "They killed him." While it shouldn't have given me pleasure to watch his pain, it did because hurting him was my only option for revenge.

"He will never have what I have." Yuri placed the gun on the table and pushed back from the desk. "This is my kingdom. I sit on the throne."

I eyed the gun and wondered if I could reach it before him. I needed to deliver another hit to his ego—his security. "You are a dead man walking. Didn't it surprise you that he came with his own security team? He's got three armed guards." I looked around. "Who's protecting you?"

"Why do you care?"

I lifted my shoulders. "I don't. All I want is to be left alone, and if telling you to empty your accounts and leave lets me walk out of here, I'm happy to do it. Not for you, but for me."

"And the filthy Italian you're sleeping with."

"Yes," I nodded, "for him too."

"What's stopping me from putting a hit on him as soon as you leave?"

"Nothing. But what's stopping me from calling Sergei as soon as I leave and telling him you're going to run?"

"I'd never run. What I should do is march up to his room and shoot him while he sleeps."

That made me laugh. I got in the door quietly, but it was only because I had seventeen years' experience of sneaking into my mother's room. Yuri wouldn't get past putting the key in the lock before either Timur or Sergei shot him.

"You do that." I picked up my bag, closed my computer and walked out the door. Never had I had a more pleasant conversation with Yuri. I didn't take a chance of walking in the open to the gate. I scurried behind the ivy and climbed the wall. If I were lucky like my real father, I'd make it back to the apartment before anyone noticed I was missing.

CHAPTER TWENTY

I opened the safe and handed weapons out like candy on Halloween.

"Yuri's got her."

Alex walked in and took the last gun from the safe. "How the hell did Yuri get her?" He removed the clip and checked the ammo. "You live in a damn fortress."

"She snuck out. I asked her about the journal. Told her we needed it to put the bastard away. She knew I'd never let her go back alone to get it. Maybe she heard my deal with Sergei."

Alex lifted his head and narrowed his eyes. "What deal?"

"I wanted to ease you into the idea that we were back in business, but seeing Katya with a gun to her head changed the plan." I stepped back as he stepped forward. For an instant, he looked as mean and foreboding as our father. One thing was certain. When his fist connected with my chin, I knew he was stronger than Vincent Wilde. Not expecting the hit, I stumbled back into the wall.

The security team around us didn't know what to do. They worked for the family and couldn't take sides, so they moved furniture and stepped back.

"You put us back into the life I worked so damn hard to get us out of?"

I was ready for the next hit. I ducked and delivered my own punch to his ribs.

"I made a deal to save Katya. It was the deal Yuri had, except now Katya would be free." Alex ran at me, and when his body hit, we fell to the floor. He had the upper hand being on top, and the first few punches hit their mark. No doubt I'd be black and blue in hours.

"My wife almost died so we could get out of the business. God, I wish I had Dad's cane right now."

The mention of Dad's cane sent a raging fire through my system. How many beatings had Alex taken for me? He had a crosshatched back to show for all the times I'd pissed Dad off and he'd stepped in to take the punishment. I owed him, so I stopped fighting and let him get in another hit or two before he realized I wasn't fighting back.

He rolled off me, and we both tried to catch our breaths. Seconds later, there was a screech from the doorway.

"What the hell is going on here?" Katya stood with her hands on her hips, scowling.

At seeing she was safe, everyone stuck the extra weapons in the safe and disappeared. I jumped to my feet and wiped the blood from my face with the edge of my T-shirt and helped Alex up from the floor.

He looked at me and shook his head. "You've got shit to straighten out." He turned his head toward Katya. "Start with her, and then figure a way to get us out of that deal with Sergei. Out means out, Matt. You can't have one foot in the mob. It's an all-or-nothing assignment." He swiped at his bloody nose and walked out of the room.

When I heard the click of the lock, I moved on Katya like tape on lint. "What the hell were you thinking?"

She pulled her bottom lip between her teeth. "I was thinking I could sneak in and sneak out and get home and be back in bed before you noticed." She reached up to touch my bleeding lip.

I pushed her hand away. "You don't get to touch me until we get this settled." I stormed by her on my way to the kitchen to get ice. I could already feel my nose getting too big for its skin. "I saw him with the gun at your head."

"Oh good, that was my plan in case you had noticed me gone."

"Oh good? That's what you have to say?"

She pulled up her jeans to show a checkerboard of bruises and reached for her own ice.

"I'm going to kill that asshole." I forgot about my injuries and tended to hers. She winced when I took my ice pack and pressed it to her shin.

"You won't have to kill him. I already did."

I stood up and looked into her eyes. "You killed Yuri?"

Her head tilted slowly from side to side. "No, I didn't actually kill him, but I started something that won't end well for him."

I lifted her from the counter and took her into the living room. Half of me wanted to turn her over my knee and spank her ass for putting herself at risk. The other half wanted to kiss the hell out of her for being here and being safe. The second half won. I pressed my lips to hers and ignored the pain. She melted into me and let out a sigh of contentment.

"I'm sorry. I just…I wanted my mother's journal. I wanted my ribbon. I wanted my damn computer."

I cupped her face and nipped at her lips. "You can't do that anymore. I'll never survive if I don't know you're safe. Promise me you won't put yourself at risk again."

"I promise I won't sneak out. I can't promise I won't be at risk. Being raised by Yuri puts me at risk, regardless. Loving you compounds it."

She was right. Being Katya Petrenko came with risks. "I love you. When I saw the gun near your head, I called in the cavalry. We were planning a coup."

She laughed. "You were going to go Scarface for me?" Her hand fell to the Glock I had tucked into the waist of my pants.

I gave her an exaggerated brow waggle. "You want to meet my little friend?"

She gripped my erection. "I wouldn't call him little."

Even though I wanted to throttle this woman, making love to her seemed the better plan. "I'm going to make you beg for me, and then we're going to talk."

She rose from the couch and walked into the bedroom. "I'm so glad you want to tackle the important stuff first."

God, I loved this girl. She was tough as nails and soft as satin, and she was mine. I made sure for the next hour she realized what she'd miss if she snuck out again. After, we showered and met at the dining room table.

"You want to tell me what your brother was talking about? What deal did you make with Sergei?"

I touched my sore nose. I hated to have to explain myself. I hated more that there was a good chance Katya would fist up and punch me too. She wanted out of this life, and my deal made sure she never would be if she stayed with me.

I really hadn't thought it through. All I wanted was a guarantee that she wouldn't have to walk down the aisle to marry the Bull.

"Before you get mad at me, I need to tell you my love for you got in the way. All I cared about when I made the deal was that you'd be free of Sergei and Yuri."

I told her what we had agreed on. She rose from her chair. Like my brother, she flew at me, but her fists didn't connect with my face. Instead, she threw herself into my lap and kissed me.

"You would have sacrificed everything for me?"

"I did sacrifice everything. That's why Alex kicked my ass."

"No one has stood up for me like that before."

"I'd die for you."

"Oh…oh…" She bounced in my lap. "I almost forgot. You no longer have a hit on you. At least not tonight." Her smile was as bright as the sun.

"You negotiated a cancellation of a hit on me?"

"Yes, I did. I got caught in the house trying to sneak out. Yuri threatened to take me to Sergei and have him dispose of me, but I told him I had dirt on Sergei that would change his life."

"What did you tell him?"

She smiled that cat and the canary type of smile. "I didn't tell him anything he didn't know. I didn't tell him what I found out that could change everything and put him back in the position of power. Yuri doesn't need to wield power over people. He's a poor leader."

Katya was talking in riddles. "What do you know?"

She wiggled in my lap, making it almost impossible to pay attention. I lifted her and sat her in her own seat. "You need to stay here, or we'll never get to the good stuff."

She stuck her lip out in a pout. "I thought I was the good stuff."

"The best. Now tell me what you've got on Sergei."

"How much would you love me if I have something so big on Sergei that it could release you from your deal?"

"I'd love you forever?"

She pursed her lips. "You're going to love me forever anyway."

"That's true, but let's pretend otherwise, and that will make you want to tell me everything."

She rose from her chair and went to the bar in the corner, grabbed a bottle of vodka and two glasses. "This is going to take a few stiff drinks."

"Oh hell, it must be good."

She poured us each a shot, and then another. It was rounding on three in the morning, and I was wide awake.

"First, you should know that I told Yuri that the Bratva wanted him dead."

"Is that true?"

She shrugged. "Does it matter? It's believable. I advised him to take his money and run."

"Will he?"

"Probably not, because he's not that smart. I'm so glad he's not my father. I hope when I find my father, he's at least got an ounce of intelligence and a pound of compassion."

I smiled because the more I looked at her, the more I saw bits of Liam in Katya, from her blue eyes to her smile, but I'd promised my brother I wouldn't say a word, and this was a promise I'd keep.

"Mafia families are different that way. We grow up hard but privileged."

She rolled her eyes. "You grew up privileged and with choices. Yuri was a dictator." She tucked her chin and mimicked his body language. "You will marry whom I choose," she said in a deep voice tinged with her accent. "You will do as I choose. You are my minion." She poured another shot and emptied it. She dropped her chin. "Not all families are like that. Look at Kirsten O'Leary. She's a veterinarian, and she probably gets to choose who she marries."

It took everything I had not to blurt that he was probably her father too. "She may be able to marry who she chooses, but she'll never marry someone who doesn't fit in her father's plans. You know the deal. They have to be on board, or they're a liability."

"Fine, back to Sergei. You know he didn't want to marry me. I'm not his type." She gave me a pageant worthy smile. "You understand what I'm saying, right?" She cupped her breasts before she moved a hand between her legs. "I'm. Not. His. Type."

"No shit?" My mind was blown. Sergei was a badass, and no one would have guessed he played for the other team. "How do you know this?"

"I caught him in the act?"

"And you're not dead?"

"I can be quiet and sneaky if I have to be."

No shit. "You're banned from room service."

"What if they only bring a tray? I love the cobbler."

I was a sucker for this woman. "Fine, but no covered tables."

"What now?" she asked.

"We call another meeting with Sergei."

CHAPTER TWENTY-ONE

Two days later, I sat in the corner booth of Gatsby's and waited for Sergei to show up. This was a private meeting. So private that Matt closed the doors and gave the bartender a long paid break and palmed him a healthy tip. On the table sat a bottle of top-shelf vodka and four glasses.

Rafe had been summoned by Alex and arrived in town yesterday. He was fresh out of school and the recipient of his license to practice law since passing his bar exam on the first try.

He and Alex argued about the sanity of meeting Sergei and Timur alone, but I knew the more who knew the truth, the less likely we'd stay alive. While Alex insisted on knowing everything, we told him nothing.

"You okay?" Matt sat at the head of a long table facing the door. I sat to his right to send a message.

"Yes, of course." I would have added I'm a Petrenko like I usually did when someone questioned my strength, but I wasn't a Petrenko. I had no idea what I was. "I'm...yours."

"And don't you ever forget that."

The door opened, and in walked the two men. Alone they were intimidating, but together they looked downright deadly. Dressed in dark suits, they moved like twins toward the table.

Matt gave me a knowing glance. This was the first time we'd seen the men and knew they were lovers. It didn't make them seem any less threatening.

Sergei sat to Matt's left, and Timur took his side to protect him. The way he circled Sergei said everything about their relationship. He would kill for him or die for him just like Matt would for me.

"What is this about? You said it was life or death." Sergei leaned forward and took in Matt's black eyes and his split lip. "Did she do that?"

"Yep, in a roundabout way she did."

"You'll look worse if you don't start talking," Sergei said.

Matt opened his mouth, but I broke in. "This is really about me, so is it okay if I start?"

He smiled and set his hand on top of mine. "Of course, my love." He winked, knowing that was how Sergei addressed me. Coming from Matt, there was conviction behind the words.

"First, I want to say it's nice to see you alive." Both of their eyes lifted. "I would have sworn that Yuri would have killed you the other night."

"He tried, but how do you know?"

I smiled. "I told him it was you or him. That the Bratva sent you to kill him."

Timur pounded the table, and Sergei soothed him softly in Russian. "You want to die too?" Sergei asked.

That was interesting language. Was it a slip or simply a translation issue?

"Too?" Matt asked.

"What stops us from taking you out right now?" Sergei pulled his gun from the holster inside his jacket and set it on the table. "It would be so easy. You didn't check us for weapons."

"There was no need," I said. "We are friends here. You used to be my fiancé. Why would I kill you?"

Matt looked to the closed door. "You're in my kingdom. You'd never make it out of here if a shot were fired. I'd prefer we have a constructive conversation that will benefit us both."

Sergei laughed. "I already have what I want from you."

I let out a heavy sigh. "About that. The deal is off the table. The Wildes are out of business."

"You do want to die, don't you?" Timur asked. It was odd for a second to break into a conversation, but Timur was more than a second. He was a partner in every sense of the word.

"No one is going to die." I reached into my back pocket to get the paper that outlined the terms of our new agreement. "Here's the new deal."

In big, bold letters on the top of the page was the sentence, *The Bratva doesn't have to know you and Timur are a couple.*

They both stared at the page, then stared at each other and then stared at Matt and me.

"Don't deny it. That would be disrespectful to your lover." I looked at Timur, whose face held the emotion of a stone. "I saw you making love to him, and it showed the passion you feel for each other."

"You watched?" Sergei asked.

I blushed. "I didn't stand there from the beginning, but I did see the end, and it's obvious you two belong together."

For the first time since Sergei walked into my life, he appeared shaken. There was a lot at stake here. "Did you tell Yuri?"

"No, I had two choices. Tell Yuri your secret or tell him the truth. I confirmed what he already knew; he was living on borrowed time. You didn't come here to be his helper. You came here to take his throne."

"You sent him to kill us?" Timur asked.

It was laughable. So much so that Matt and I both laughed. "No, I left him in his office knowing you killed my brother and that he was next."

Sergei didn't deny responsibility for Mikhail's death. "What do you want?"

I sat taller. Who knew I'd take on the position of power? "The Wildes are out. You deal with Yuri; we don't want to know what happens to him. For all I know, he took his resources and ran."

Timur smirked. "He did run. He didn't get very far."

That told me everything I needed to know. "Then it's settled. I will keep your secret. You will keep us safe." I threaded my fingers through Matt's. "We want a normal life."

Sergei shook his head. "You'll never escape the wrath of the Russian mafia."

I pressed the note forward and pointed to the line that read, *Only Matt and I know your truth. It will stay a secret as long as we are safe.*

"You're wrong. It's in your best interests to make sure we do because I've made arrangements for the truth to be revealed if anything were to happen to any of the Wildes."

Sergei sat back and rubbed the scruff on his chin. "I imagine you'll be a Wilde soon."

I looked at Matt. "Who knows, he hasn't asked."

He squeezed my hand. There was no doubt he'd get there eventually. He'd already branded me with his love.

"What else do you want?" Timur asked.

"Nothing."

They sat back and twisted their heads to the side like confused puppies. "You don't want the house? The assets?"

I leaned into Matt. "I've got everything I want right here."

"We have a problem." Sergei leaned forward like he was divulging a secret. "Your father…I mean Yuri took an extended vacation." He looked at me. "I've been told that while your skills are amateur at best," he looked at Matt, "your fiancé has the skills to access the finances I'll need to take over."

I wasn't sure who to punch first. Sergei, who insinuated my hacking skills were subpar, or Matt, who fed him that bullshit.

"You want everything?" Matt asked

Sergei and Timur nodded. "Of course," they said in unison.

I opened the bottle of vodka that sat on the table and poured four shots. "The money is easy, but we will need a lawyer willing to falsify records if you want the house and properties."

"I want it all," Sergei replied.

"Then you shall have it." I looked at Matt. "Can your brother do the paperwork?" The furrow in his forehead told me he wasn't sure that was a good idea. Everything came down to transferring ownership, and the fewer people who knew, the better, so in my mind, that meant keep it in the family.

"I'll see what I can do. Shall we seal it with a drink?"

I rose and raised my glass. "To those who have our hearts. May they have our backs as well."

Every one pounded back the shot, and we all walked to the door, where there were no less than six goons waiting on the other side.

Sergei's men stood stoic and proud while Matt's men analyzed their every move. When they saw all of us walk out blood-free, there was a collective nod. Today, no one would die.

Sergei turned to Matt. "If she ever hits you again, I hear that filthy leprechaun O'Leary has a daughter who can stitch you up. At least the Irish bastard contributes something."

"I'll keep that in mind." Matt laughed all the way back to the apartment.

"What's gotten into you?"

"Nothing. I just find his aversion to the Irish funny. It will be interesting to see how this all pans out."

I opened the door to the apartment to find Rafe and Alex pacing the living room. Stella and Faye were in the kitchen, and the smell of something wonderful filled the air.

"How'd it go?" Rafe picked up his beer and emptied the bottle before he took another from the iced bucket on the coffee table.

Matt nodded but didn't say much.

"Your silence means there's a hitch in the plan.

Since we aren't privy to the damn plan, we don't know how to help. Why can't we know?"

"Because it keeps you safe," I said. "I'm going to help the girls." I turned to walk away but heard Alex speak.

"Information is power. We need to know."

"No, but I need something from you."

I looked over my shoulder to Rafe, whose eyes grew as wide as a full moon. "Me? No way. I'm out. In fact, I was never in. I refuse to put my license on the line because you're a damn ass." He looked at me and added, "And whipped."

In the kitchen, I started filling plastic baggies with ice cubes.

Faye came over to help. "Is someone hurt?"

"Not yet. Wait a minute."

CHAPTER TWENTY-TWO

I put the couch between me and my brothers to save my face, not save face. Katya and I made the best deal we could. I wasn't ashamed of what we accomplished when it could have gone the other way. This wasn't perfect, but it was the hand I was dealt, and I intended to make everyone a winner.

"I need one thing, and it's all over."

"No," Alex said. "No deal. Rafe is the only one who hasn't been damaged by Dad and his dealings. Don't be the one who changes that. There's no rewind or restart in this life. He's managed to come out clean. Let him stay that way."

"Can we sit down and talk about this? I need

one thing. It's not that big of a deal. Once I deliver this one thing to Sergei, we are out for good." I stared at the cushions on the couch and debated whether I should sit or run.

Rafe flopped into the chair while Alex fell into the sofa. I took the safe route and sat on the sofa arm as far away from both of my brothers as possible.

I ignored Alex and looked at Rafe. "It's simple paperwork."

"How simple, and what kind of paperwork?" Rafe twisted the cap off his beer and took a long pull.

"No way. He's not doing anything." Alex raised his voice.

Faye peeked around the corner. "Anyone need ice?"

"Or Band-Aids?" Katya added.

They both stood in the doorway and watched for a minute. When no one asked for first aid, they went back to the kitchen.

Rafe got up and paced the room. He looked at Alex. "I'll do it."

"I said no." Alex rose.

I moved back behind the sofa.

Rafe frowned. "You don't get to choose. While

I'm not thrilled about losing my license after going to school for years, I realize I've never paid my dues for this family." He grabbed a third beer and twisted the cap. The hiss of carbonation broke the silence. "Dad sent me to law school for this. He wanted me to represent our family when we were in trouble. I was supposed to be the secret weapon. But how good is the weapon if you never fire it?"

"No," Alex repeated.

Rafe challenged him. "You don't get to decide for all of us. I'll do it this one time, but don't ever ask me to break the law again."

"How do you know I'm asking you to break the law?" I asked.

"Come on, you're a Wilde, and lawlessness runs in your veins. I know you're not asking me to draw up a will."

I laughed. "You're not too far off the mark."

While Alex sat and scowled at us, I told Rafe what we'd need to exit our life of crime for good.

"Give me a week. I'll have it ready, but don't ever ask me to help again. I love you, and I understand you love Katya, but I don't get it. No woman is worth this. However, we are family, and family is worth everything."

Rafe left Alex and me in the living room. I wasn't certain I'd avoided an ass kicking until he asked, "Did you get the hair?"

And that's how the subject of Sergei ended and Liam began. I rushed to the bathroom and plucked the hair from the tile. I emptied the baggie of water that held ice days ago and put the single strand inside. When I returned, everyone was moving toward the dining room. On a big platter sat Stella's pot roast Italian style.

Out of respect for me, Alex left the seat at the head of the table open. As I walked by him, I slid the baggie into his jacket pocket. The rest of the night was spent the way it should be, dining with my family and making love to my fiancée. Or soon to be fiancée; all I needed was the ring and a yes.

THE NEXT DAY, I left Katya asleep in bed. My poor girl hadn't gotten much rest in days, and last night was no exception. Once my family left, we popped a bottle of champagne and celebrated our good luck.

I was still angry that she'd snuck out of the house, but without that information about Sergei and Timur, my family would have been trapped into a life of crime. There was one more hurdle to clear, and that was coming to terms with Katya's heritage. Here was a woman born Russian, who would marry Italian, and was really Irish if my gut feeling was right.

While she slept, I read her mother's journal and wanted to weep for her. My mother always said that life was preordained, which meant that everything that happened was for a reason. What if I was the reason Katya's mother died and she was forced to stay in Las Vegas? If I was preordained to be hers, I had a lot to make up for because my woman suffered plenty while she waited for me.

Stella was in the kitchen when I walked in. "Is she ready for breakfast?"

I kissed her on the cheek because she was always there for me. "No. She's sleeping. It's been a taxing couple of weeks for her."

Stella nodded. "Your mother would have liked her."

"Do you like her?" It was important to me that Stella approve, but if she didn't, I would still choose Katya because she was my future.

"I do. She's strong and sensitive. She'll make a good mother. She'll be a lioness and a kitten."

The thought of our children warmed my insides. I'd been hoping to plant my seed inside Katya this whole time so when I proposed, she couldn't possibly say no, but those thoughts were dashed when she told me we were safe because she had the shot. I made a commitment that day to make sure she missed her next appointment.

"She's a good woman."

Stella smiled. "And I'm plumping her up for you."

I laughed. Stella once told me that a skinny girl was a waste of time. Dating one was like milking a bull. "You're doing well in that department." I'd noticed that Katya's stomach and hips had rounded. Her thighs cushioned my hips when settled between them. Her breast had barely filled my fingers but now filled my hands. "She loves your pancakes."

"I shall make them now. Where are you off to this morning?"

I gave her a hug. "To buy a ring and make her mine."

"Make it big."

I kissed her cheek again. "You want everything plump."

She smiled and went back to cooking.

I visited at least a dozen jewelry stores before

I found the perfect setting. It was a massive square yellow diamond set in a halo of smaller diamonds. It was far from traditional, but it was unique and named fire and ice, which was exactly how I saw my future wife.

While she would always have the cold Siberian edge from her Russian side, she also had the warmth of another running through her veins.

When I got home, I found Katya in the closet. She stood looking at a white dress. "Did you buy a new dress?" I came behind her and kissed her neck.

"No, this was supposed to be my wedding dress to Sergei." She reached out and touched the soft fabric. "I hated that I had to buy it."

I reached for the hanger. "Let's get rid of it."

"No, while I didn't want to marry Sergei, I do love this dress."

"It's perfect, then." I turned her around and kissed her before I dropped to one knee. "I didn't expect to do this in the closet, but does it matter where I ask you to be mine forever?"

Her blues brightened, if that was even possible. "Are you...?"

I took her right hand in mine and kissed it. "I am, so listen carefully because I don't want there to be any confusion." I took the little white box from my pocket and listened to her gasp. "Katya Anya, will you be my partner in love and life? Will you stay with me through thick and thin? Will you have my children and my heart?"

"Ask the real question, Matteo."

I opened the box to show the diamond I'd chosen for her. "Will you marry me?" I waited and waited while she stared at the ring. "This is when you say ye—"

She dropped to her knees and kissed me. "Yes, a thousand times, yes."

I placed the ring on her finger. No one would mistake her for single ever again. "You've got the ring and the dress. I can have us married in an hour."

She looked down at her finger. "It's perfect, but I have to wait. I have a father who doesn't know I exist. I want to give him a chance to be a father if he chooses. A father should give his daughter away the right way. With her permission. Can we wait until I can at least give finding him an honest chance?"

How could I deny her? While an hour from now sounded better to me, I knew the wait wouldn't be long. Alex had put a rush on the results, and it would only be days until we knew for certain.

"Yes, sweetheart. We'll wait for your father. I have a feeling he's going to be thrilled to know you."

CHAPTER TWENTY-THREE

When I tried on my dress, it no longer fit. Stella giggled and fed me another plate of pancakes. "That's an easy fix," she told me.

An hour later, the dress was gone with a promise to be back by nightfall. Not that I needed it anytime soon. I refused to get married until I had made a genuine effort to find my real father. Without much to go on, I'd hit a dead end.

While I knew of many powerful men in Las Vegas, I was not on a first name basis with any, and certainly not on a nickname basis. Lucky could have been anyone in a town known for luck. For all I knew, he could have been my mother's masseuse since she met him at the spa.

Matt walked out of our bedroom looking

quite handsome in his suit and tie. He leaned over and gave me a kiss. "I'm off to get the paperwork settled."

"Rafe got it taken care of?" I knew he wasn't happy to forge documents, but he agreed as his one contribution as a member of the infamous Wilde family. As a new lawyer at McAlister and Associates, this was the kind of work Rafe would be assigned along with every two-bit criminal who walked through the door, so it was easy enough for him to file the paperwork and put it on a partner's desk for signature. As long as the fee for services was paid, no one would give it a second thought.

"He's got it all done. We have a look-alike to walk in and pretend they're Yuri, so in case anyone asks, there's proof he was there."

It was amazing how much Matt and his brothers were willing to do to protect me. That was what family was supposed to be like.

"You guys went the extra mile."

"It's got to work for everyone, including Sergei, or we are back at the beginning."

Sergei had done everything he was asked. He stayed away from Old Money Casino. He ceased putting pressure on Matt to continue the deal. Every time I looked over my shoulder, I saw one of his men. They weren't there to harm me. They were there to make sure I was safe because my safety and Sergei's went hand in hand.

"Be careful. There are bigger issues than Sergei." Rumor had it the Colombians were flexing their muscles, and since the Wildes left the business, it created a vacuum everyone was jockeying to fill. Given the two big players were still the Russians and the Irish, I'd put my money on Sergei. Any man who stayed under the Bratva's radar and moved up in rank to take over had skill and luck. He'd made Yuri completely disappear without question. I had questions for sure, but I was smart enough not to ask. What I didn't know couldn't hurt me.

"Stella made you an appointment at the spa. Happy Birthday, sweetheart. We have a celebratory dinner planned tonight."

He was such a funny man who made a big deal out of everything, but if he wanted to celebrate, I'd be a happy reveler.

"Is it just you and I?"

He smiled. "It's a private affair." He lifted my hand to his lips and kissed my ring as if I were the Pope. I think he simply liked seeing it on my finger. It was as good as a tattoo on my forehead that said I was his. "Wear that red dress I love."

I watched him walk out the door. It didn't take long for Stella to fill the void Matt left behind. "What's your favorite flower?" she asked.

"That's easy. I love roses."

She smiled and walked out of the room, no doubt to fill the apartment with their fragrant scent.

I walked to the living room and took a seat on the sofa. Had it really only been weeks since I moved here? The anniversary of my mother's death came and went. I'd brought her favorite roses to the cemetery and told her how much I loved her. I sat on the grass and read her diary again. I released all the guilt I felt at having been angry because she'd killed herself. I'd asked her forgiveness because I only knew what I'd been told. I knew she was with me when a light breeze caressed my skin. I swore I heard the whisper of her voice on the wind tell me how much she missed me.

My wedding day to Sergei passed without much thought. I would have completely forgotten about it had it not been for the priest calling to confirm the date and me telling him the wedding was off. He sounded almost relieved.

Today was my twenty-fifth birthday, and my life had changed in profound ways. I slept with the man I'd dreamed of all my life. I no longer had family ties to the Russian mafia. My loyalties were with the Wildes. Soon, if I had an ounce of my true father's luck, I'd find my real family. Would he be married? Would I have sisters or brothers? Would they embrace me or treat me like the outsider I'd been in the Petrenko household? My hopes were high that I'd be something more. "You need to go to your appointment," Stella said. "Get going before you're late." If the older Italian woman wasn't force feeding me, she was bossing me around, but I loved her motherly instincts. It had been far too long to be without a mother's love.

I picked up my bag and walked out the door. "You ready?" Sophie asked. She was my personal detail. Matt had handpicked her himself. He liked that she was female and trained by the Israelis. I liked that she was rarely seen. She managed to blend in with the woodwork. I knew she was around, but I never felt suffocated.

"I'm ready."

It was odd that I'd been unsupervised my entire life until now. I never realized how much danger lurked in the shadows. I had always been a target, and yet Yuri never thought to protect me because I was nothing to him. And now I was everything to Matt.

We took the elevator down to the spa. The second the receptionist saw me, I was ushered into a private room where for the next three hours I was exfoliated, moisturized, waxed, painted, styled and made up. I truly felt beautiful.

When I arrived back in the apartment, my red dress was laid out for me, as were the shoes to match.

The dress had fallen over my hips just as Matt walked in.

"You take my breath away." He walked up behind me, pushed my hair to the side and kissed my neck. Goosebumps danced across my skin. How I ever thought I'd be able to make love to this man once and get him out of my system was insane. Energy pulsed below the surface of my skin when he was near. He was as necessary to my survival as oxygen and Stella's pancakes.

"You are my breath."

He zipped up the back of my dress and turned me around. "Happy Birthday." He pulled a white box from his pocket and held it out in his open palm. "I bought you something I hope you'll love."

"I already love it because you picked it out."

"Open it. It's special and has significant meaning."

I'd gone years without anyone acknowledging my birthday. It felt almost wrong to have a gift in my hand. When I didn't open the box, Matt did. On a bed of white satin sat a pair of emerald earrings in the shape of a four-leaf clover.

"It's the symbol of luck."

I put them on. "I don't need luck. I've got you."

"Yes, you do." He lifted one of the dangling earrings and smiled. "Let's get lucky." He threaded his fingers through mine and led me out the door.

"Where are we going?"

He chuckled. "Lucky Luciano's, of course." It was the high-end Italian eatery in the casino.

"Are you trying to make me Italian by ingestion?" I'd eaten more Italian food in the last three weeks than I'd eaten in my entire life.

"No, I'll make you Italian by insemination. I'm just going with a theme tonight."

I laughed. "Lucky is the theme? I'm pretty sure you're going to get lucky tonight."

He patted my ass as we walked to the elevator. "No, baby, it's *you* who's getting lucky tonight."

We entered the elevator alone, and he kissed me until the doors opened on the first floor.

When Matt walked through the casino, it was like magic. He was the star, and nothing short of red carpet and paparazzi would do. Everyone knew him, and by association, they knew me.

When we got to Lucky Luciano's, there was a sign on the door that said closed for a private party.

"You shut down the restaurant for me?"

He grabbed the handle of the door and waited. "Tonight is far too special to share it with anyone else."

"It's just a birthday."

He brushed his lips against mine. "It's so much more than that."

He opened the door, and on the tables were my mother's favorite roses—one pink, one yellow and one white. Two were named after Diana, the Princess of Wales. Even my mother believed in fairy tales.

Petals on the floor led us to a table in the back. I stopped when I saw a man sitting with his back to us. His strawberry blond hair seemed familiar, and yet not.

"Someone's at our table," I whispered to Matt.

"Yes. It's a surprise."

My breath caught in my throat. The theme was lucky because he'd found my father. My knees grew week. I gripped Matt's arm. "You found him."

He cupped my cheeks. "Yes."

"How do you know for sure?"

He reached up and plucked a hair from my head. He held it in front of me. "You share his DNA."

I sucked in a huge breath. "You knew, then."

"I wasn't sure, but I was motivated to find out. If all goes well, you'll be a Wilde tomorrow."

My mouth dropped open. "Tomorrow?"

He smiled. "You told me you couldn't marry me until you found your father. He's here, and he's excited to get reacquainted with you."

He said reacquainted which meant I'd already met him. I stared at the man, who slowly rose from his chair and turned around. He was none other than Liam O'Leary. Lucky O'Leary.

"Oh my God. I'm Irish." I rushed forward and hugged my father for the first time.

He stood back and took me in. "I always thought you were far too pretty to be Yuri's daughter," he said with a heavy brogue.

I straightened my shoulders and stood tall. "Of course. I'm Katya Anya, and I look like my mother."

He pulled me in for a hug. "Yes, you do. Your mother owned my heart."

We sat at the table and caught up on the twenty-five years he'd missed. He said he'd loved my mother but respected her decision to stay with Mikhail. When she told him she was pregnant again with Yuri's child, she felt it was best if they quit their affair.

"Your mother was a brave woman, but she was also a mother, and she loved Mikhail too much to leave him in the hands of Yuri." He wiped at a tear. "I never knew you were mine. She never told me. I would have—"

I placed my hand on my father's. "She was trying to protect us both. She took the secret to her grave."

Liam's cheeks grew beet red. "When I find Yuri, I'm going to kill him."

Matt and I looked at each other and smiled. "He's no longer a problem, we're told."

Liam lifted his bushy brows. "Who do I need to thank?"

I giggled. With the way Sergei felt about the Irish, I didn't expect that meeting to go well. "Sergei Volkov, I imagine."

My father frowned and grumbled something about big Russian oafs and small brains.

He leaned over and took something from the empty seat beside him.

"It's not much, but I think you'll love it." He slid the beautifully wrapped package across the table to me.

I opened the box that was tied with a red ribbon, and inside I found a photo album. I opened the first page to a picture of my mother and Liam. They stood in a rose garden, looking happier than any two people I'd ever seen.

"You are the reason she loved roses so much?" It was more of a question than a statement.

"She loved the gardens in Caesar's Palace. We met there all the time or at the spa."

I touched the picture as if it would somehow bring her back, and in a way, it did because this was the only picture I had of my mother. I flipped through the pages and saw the light of love shine from her eyes in each picture. There were some of her alone and some of her with Liam. There was one of her and him with his three children. It occurred to me that I indeed had siblings.

"Do they know?"

He nodded. "Yes, and they are happy to invite you into the family. It's odd for them. It may take some time to get used to having a new sister, but they're open to the idea. They only met your mother once. It wasn't planned; we just happened to be at the same place having lunch. "You were there too." He pointed to my mother's pregnant stomach.

I looked at the picture closely. "Wow, we were actually together as a family."

"Yes, we were, but no one knew."

I stared at my siblings. Kirsten was a small child. I knew her mother had died at her birth. Ian and Patrick stood on each side of her as if she were theirs to protect. How much I'd missed.

"I look forward to seeing them."

My father looked at Matt and frowned. "You'll see them tomorrow at your wedding."

My eyes grew wide as I snapped my head around to Matt. "You were serious. We're getting married tomorrow?"

Matt reached for my hands and brought them to his lips. "I don't want to wait another minute. Haven't we wasted enough time?"

He was right. I'd pined for him my whole life and put him off until my father could be found, and now that he was here, there was no reason to wait.

Liam looked at Matt. "As your father, I'd be failing you if I didn't tell you that you could do better than this Italian, but as my daughter and the daughter of Anya, I know you're choosing with your heart and not your head. It would be my pleasure to walk you down the aisle if you'd like."

I leaped up and threw my hands around Liam's neck. "Yes, I want you to give me away."

He pet my hair like I was a puppy. "I just got you back. I'll never give you away again, but I will loan you to this man, provided he takes care of you." He gave Matt a hard look. "Son, if you don't, you'll have to answer to me."

"Yes, sir. I will spend every minute of the rest of my life keeping Katya happy."

Liam rose. "Make sure you do." He gave me a kiss and told me he'd see me tomorrow and then walked away.

"I don't know if I should hit you or kiss you."

A waiter arrived with our first course.

"Oh sweetheart, eat up because you're going to be kissing me all night long."

CHAPTER TWENTY-FOUR

The Wilde name came with money and power. I stood at the altar of the church and waited for my bride. They say it takes a village to raise a child. It took a city to plan a wedding any woman would love, and it took less than twenty-four hours to get it to all come together.

I stood proudly next to my brother Rafe, who put his dreams at risk so I could live mine.

"You can turn and run. I mean, you're marrying into the Irish mafia. How is that going to play into your plan of legitimacy?"

While he talked to me, his eyes never left the front pew, where Kirsten O'Leary sat. Maybe my marriage to Katya would bridge the gap between the two families. Liam couldn't hate the Wildes too much if his daughter was married to one.

"Still have a thing for the little shamrock, do ya?"

"Don't let her hear you call her that. She'd gut you in a second."

"Euthanize me, maybe. Her specialty is animals."

Rafe looked at me. "Like I was saying. And no, I don't have a thing for Kirsten. Even if I did, Ian would kill me right after her father castrated me. I'm not interested in anyone right now."

"Right." I knew he'd had a thing for her ever since they were in school together.

The music began to play, and my heart started at a gallop and continued to race until my head grew dizzy. A month ago, I would have told anyone I'd have a higher likelihood of getting gunned down than married. Hell, a month ago, getting gunned down sounded far more appealing, but as I watched the aisle of the mostly empty church and saw my brother and best man Alex lead his wife and Katya's bridesmaid down the aisle, I realized marrying Katya would be my smartest decision.

Alex kissed his wife and left her on the opposite side of the aisle before he joined me. Seconds later, the double doors opened and Katya and Liam appeared. He stood proudly as he walked her down the aisle. Dressed in a black tuxedo embellished with a four-leaf clover cummerbund, he walked the most beautiful woman alive toward me.

I couldn't take my eyes off her. The white dress she had chosen was perfect to showcase her long, sexy legs. The light coming from the back of the church circled her like a divine light.

When they got to the front of the church, I walked to the center to meet her.

"You didn't run," she said when I stood in front of her.

"Not a chance."

Liam cleared his throat. "I can still fix you up with a nice Irish boy."

Katya cupped his cheek and smiled. "Thank you, but I chose him."

Liam nodded and waited for the priest to ask who gave this woman to be married. He proudly announced to everyone that he, Liam O'Leary, would give his daughter to marry Matteo Wilde.

There was a bit of commotion coming from the pews. We all turned to watch Sergei. Katya and I laughed. We had forgotten to tell him about her true heritage.

Liam walked away and sat with his sons and daughter.

The priest went through all the motions. He said all the words. I never heard one of them. The words didn't matter. All that I cared about was this woman and the kiss that would seal the deal. When asked if she'd take me as her husband, her 'yes' wasn't soft or subdued. She said it loud enough for her mother to hear in heaven or Yuri to hear in hell.

I was already kissing her before the priest gave us permission, but Katya and I would never be traditionalists. This was our life, and we'd live it by our rules. Our new motto was 'take no prisoners'.

After the ceremony, we all converged on Capones, where the alcohol flowed freely and the music played all night.

Kirsten, Ian, and Patrick welcomed my wife to their family with a hug. They gave me a handshake and a warning to keep Katya happy or else.

In the corner sat Rafe by himself. I felt sorry for my brother, who grew up as a good man in a gangster's universe. I followed his line of sight to Kirsten, who danced with her brother Ian.

There was no chance for them in our world—a world where marriage was a calculated bet. Where love was a bonus and not a guarantee. Where an Irish mob princess would never be allowed to marry my Italian brother. Then again, this was Las Vegas, and anything was possible.